John P. Prendergast

**Ireland from the Restoration to the Revolution**

1660-1690

John P. Prendergast

**Ireland from the Restoration to the Revolution**
*1660-1690*

ISBN/EAN: 9783337227258

Printed in Europe, USA, Canada, Australia, Japan

Cover: Foto ©Andreas Hilbeck / pixelio.de

More available books at **www.hansebooks.com**

# IRELAND

FROM THE

## RESTORATION TO THE REVOLUTION,

### 1660 to 1690.

BY

### JOHN P. PRENDERGAST,

AUTHOR OF "THE CROMWELLIAN SETTLEMENT."

LONDON:
LONGMANS, GREEN, AND CO.,
1887.

# PREFACE.

—⊸⊱⊰⊶—

Ormonde likens the Restoration to the resurrection, "when God, beyond our hope (he says), took us all from banishment, dispersion, and out of the lowest and most comfortless degree of despair, and restored us to our country, to our fortune, and to our friends."[1] However true this statement might be for himself and his family it left the great body of his countrymen deprived of their lands, who by the Peace of '48, contracted by himself by the authority of King Charles I., and adopted and confirmed by Charles II., were to be pardoned and restored.

A good deal of the secret history of this transaction not mentioned by Carte, though he had all the documents before him, is now disclosed. For Carte wrote a eulogy of Ormonde.

But Ormonde confesses that Ireland was sold to the Cromwellians, on the ground, no doubt, that thus only could the King and the royalists be restored.

" If others can (says Ormonde), I cannot forget our many years wandering abroad, and what we promised

---

[1] To the Countess of Clancarty on the Earl of Clancarty's death. Dated Moore Park, this 5th of August, 1665. Carte's Life of Ormonde, III. 122.

to get home, and if not to break those promises be to want resolution and vigour, I am glad I am without them."[1]

But this confession left him liable to the charge of neglecting the interests of those that fought in his army under his own command in Ireland in 1649 and 1650, and in Spain, France, and Flanders, under the King's Ensigns for seven years from 1652 to 1659, called Ensignmen, as well as those named specially for restoration by the King for reasons known to himself, called Nominees or Mero Motu men—who were to be pardoned and restored by the articles of the Peaces of 1646 and 1648.

A work on the Restoration Settlement of Ireland is of more importance even than the Cromwellian Settlement ; and there are more abundant materials for its elucidation.

But the history of Ireland is distasteful to the English public.

By the King's Declaration for the Settlement of Ireland of 30th November, 1660, there was an elaborate scheme produced making provision for all classes of the Irish, some for restoration, as the Innocents, some for deprivation as the Nuncio-tists and the rejecters of the Peaces of 1646 and 1648. But all except Innocents were only to be restored after reprisals found for the Cromwellians in possession.

---

[1] Ormonde to his nephew James Hamilton, ancestor of the Aberoorn family. November 21st, 1663. C. P. xlix. 162.

And as there were no reprisals forthcoming there could be no restoration. . . . . .

The King's Declaration of 30th November, 1660, made when the Cromwellians did not know their strength, deals in very different terms with the Irish than at the end of two years when the Act of Settlement was passed. In the Declaration the King and his subjects are restored to each other with wonderful circumstances of affection and confidence.[1] But the Act of Settlement which confirms the Declaration meets the reader with a preamble magnifying the Rebellion and Massacre, and glorifying the victory of the King's English Protestant subjects as a victory and conquest over Irish rebels and enemies, so that their liberties and lands were wholly at His Majesty's disposal.[2]

The conduct of the Thirty-six Commissioners for executing the King's Declaration of Settlement having discredited the Declaration by their partiality, a new Court under five English Commissioners was opened, limited to one year, for hearing claims of Innocence to the number of over 8,000. But after sitting and hearing one-sixth of the claimants during seven months, the previous five months being occupied in framing rules and waiting for the printing of the Act, the Court of Innocents was closed on the 21st of August,

---

[1] King's Declaration of 30th November, 1660. Clause I.
[2] Preamble to Act of Settlement, passed 27th September, 1662.

1663, and remained so till January, 1666, when a new Court of Claims was opened for Protestants or English only (unless a few Irish Proviso-men), with a limit of three years to hear Adventurers, Soldiers, and Proviso-men.

The details of the Act of Settlement is a subject of vast complexity ; and still wants an historian. Without elucidation it leaves the history of Ireland a riddle.

The Restoration Settlement of Ireland might well be described as a Tragedy in three acts. The King's Declaration of 30th November 1660, might be described as the first act. Here all is fair and hope-ful. Then comes the Act of Settlement of 27th September, 1662, treating the Irish as conquered enemies, with their lands at the disposal of the conquerors. But the rights of Innocents were still acknowledged, and the binding force of the Peace and other engagements. Last, at the end of more than three years, comes the Act of Explanation, shutting the door of hope on all Innocents unheard—on the Article-men or those claiming the conditions of the Peace of 1648— on the Ensign-men and the Nominees.

The following lines from a poem addressed to the Duke of Ormonde, under the title of a Naval Allegory, by the Registrar of the Irish Court of Admiralty, on his fourth Lieutenancy of Ireland in 1677, may give some idea of the many interests involved in the Acts of Settlement and Explanation. After some lines concerning

Ormonde's earlier Lieutenancies, he compares his
career to the course of a ship

> " Amidst a thousand rocks. There lay a sand
> Of souldiers' interest (some in command,
> Some out). There a dangerous shelfe
> Of vext Adventurers and men of pelfe.
> Here a strange tide of Innocents sett in,
> Which spoiled the fishing, Nocents were so thin.
> There Connaught purchasers and transplantees,
> Meeting a thousand sort of bold grantees
> Made a ground sea. Here came a hazy fog
> Of dark provisos which the Act did clog.
> There arose clouds of several sorts of men
> (Whose names I can't remember one in ten)
> Ensigne—Mero motu—Men reprizable—
> Nominees—and such as never yet were able
> To set their foot on land.——
>
> &ast; &ast; &ast; &ast; &ast; &ast;
>
> Thus we all though late
> Came to an anchor in Certificate ;
> When having stayed a tide, at length we went
> All safe ashore in Letters called Pattènt.
> Some of the fleet stayed in the bay Decree,
> Some hall'd in the open road of Letteree."[1]

At a time when nothing less than a new Settlement
of Landed Property in Ireland is contemplated by
some, it may be instructive to review some of the
miseries involved in the Settlement at the Restoration.
It is to be hoped that what is here detailed, may make

[1] C. P. lxix, 553.

those pause who have embraced in their minds any such ruinous resolutions.

The Cromwellian Settlement, confirmed to a great extent by the Acts of Settlement, left the country convulsed by the social revolution it effected, and is responsible in a great degree for its present condition.

The Old English, foreign by race but of the same religion as the Irish, and called by some the Later or Newer Irish, the Butlers, Plunkets, Fitzgeralds, and others, were all swept into Connaught with the Old Irish, and there perished for the most part, and thus the connecting link between the two races on the soil of Ireland was destroyed.

In the place of these later Irish another race of the same religion has grown up and become landed proprietors through thrift, and is likely to supply the lost link. But if they too are to be swept away and a new settlement of landed property attempted, Ireland will be in the condition of always settling but never settled.

Mr. Gladstone attempted by an heroic effort to settle Ireland on the Ulster principle of the three F's, Fixity of Tenure, Fair Rents, and Free Sale. But his measures seem only to have unsettled Ireland, and headstrong men are urging on another social revolution, with the view of driving out of the island the only class accustomed to government. If they ground their argument on the Cromwellian Settlement, it is an event of over two hundred years' antiquity, and the common fate of Europe in the dark ages, that of Ireland in the time of Cromwell being no different from the rest only in being the latest. It must be always remembered that the present landlords of Ireland had no hand in the Cromwellian Conquest—that they rely on the public faith of the Kingdom expressed in various Acts of the Legislature—that Englishmen have given their daughters to Irishmen in reliance on that settlement of property, that Millions of money have been lent upon it, and that to undo it now would be a gross breach of faith, and cause Ireland to remain unsettled perhaps for ages.

# TABLE OF CONTENTS.

## PART I.

### CHAPTER 1.

## PART II.

### CHAPTER I.

# CHAPTER IV.

## CONNAUGHT TORIES.

# CHAPTER V.

## THE ULSTER TORIES.

## PART III.

### CHAPTER I.

## Contents.

## CHAPTER II.

## CHAPTER III.

# IRELAND

FROM THE

## RESTORATION TO THE REVOLUTION,

### A.D. 1660–1690.

———◆———

CHAPTER I.

THE UNSETTLED STATE OF IRELAND AT THE
RESTORATION.

IN July, 1662, the Duke of Ormonde came over as
Lord Lieutenant to administer the affairs of Ireland,
"as divided and unsettled a country (to use his own
expression), as is or ever was in Christendom." By
the scheme of the Parliament of England, the former
Irish proprietors had been swept from the three other
provinces into Connaught, and their ancient properties
were divided amongst the Cromwellian soldiery. The
lands of Royalist Protestants had been some of them
compounded for at two years' purchase, some set out
among the soldiery. The owners of others were
banished like Ormonde, Bramhall, and Sir James Montgomery, together with the chief Catholic Irish leaders
who had been Commanders in the war against the
Parliament.

The Protestant hierarchy was abolished, and the
Bishops' and Rectors' lands set out among the
Cromwellians.

At the Restoration the Protestants were at once
restored.

                                          A

The Irish had to use their influence at Court to obtain the King's order under Privy Seal for their repossession.

The Irish Officers, the King's comrades in his ten years' exile, who had rallied to his ensigns, and given him credit and dignity by fighting as his soldiers in the armies of France and Spain, where they made up a force of ten thousand men, crowded to Whitehall and pressed him for Letters of Restoration to their lands. Ormonde, Inchiquin, Anglesey, and other grandees were at this early stage willing to give certificates of the services and sufferings of many of these officers. With these they made their way to their old homes; and in many instances got them back;—for the Cromwellians had no legal title. They had only the King's Proclamation of 29th May, 1660, commanding that they should not be disturbed until further order should be given in Parliament. The King's order under Privy Seal to restore any Irish proprietor seemed of equal validity with the Proclamation. This roused the ire of the Cromwellians. A meeting was held in Cashel in August, 1660, by Colonel Thomas Stanley, Colonels Richard and Peyton Le Hunte and others, for adopting a petition by the Cromwellians of the county of Tipperary, " dispersed with great success, they said, through the whole kingdom."

It asked for a Parliament to confirm their titles. They were alarmed at the number of officers of high quality flocking from abroad, and, notwithstanding the murders and cruelties done to multitudes of the petitioners' dear brethren, these officers of quality would have themselves to be accounted the King's best subjects ; and not seeming to question, they added, their restitution to their estates so justly forfeited. On these, the officers and soldiers had laid out their all (so ran this petition or declaration), hoping for the comfortable settlement of themselves and their posterity. It was by mere accident that they had not got the qualification of a Parliamentary title.

They forwarded this petition or declaration to Colonel Symon Finch, at Kilcolman, near Nenagh, that he and his soldiers, planted around him in his barony, might sign it ; and to their good friends Bartholomew Fookes, and the rest in the barony of Eliogarty and Ikerrin. It was signing, they added, by multitudes of the Protestant inhabitants, as well officers civil and military, as adventurers, soldiers and other planters.

On the other hand, the dispossessed Irish, as their hopes of restoration began to fail, with wives, sons, and daughters around them starving, were furnishing recruits to the bands of tories that, since Cromwell's time, had gathered in wilds and woods avenging their wrongs on the possessors of their former properties.

So that Ormonde might well describe Ireland as the most divided and unsettled country in Christendom. For nothing in the history of Europe was similar to the Cromwellian Settlement, except the Conquests effected by the Northern barbarians in the dark ages If Augustin Thierry had known the true story of the Cromwellian Settlement, he need not have selected the Conquest of England by the Normans for its being the latest of those conquests, where men deprived of all that makes life valuable, are seen either resigning themselves to the sight of strangers sitting as masters at hearths that had been lately theirs, or frantic with despair and rage, rushing to the mountains or the forests to live there in rapine, murder, and independence.[1]

Generals, colonels, captains, and lieutenants of the Parliamentary forces now claimed the ancient castles of the royalists and native nobility and gentry of Ireland as the residences and property of themselves and their families.   Or an Adventurer—some merchant of London, or tradesman from a provincial town in England—had set himself down with his wife and children, and servants, in what had lately, and long before been, the home of some old English family of the birth of Ireland ; some Butler, Fitzgerald, or Plunket, or of some nobleman or gentleman, Irish by both birth and blood ; some Kavanagh, M'Carthy, O'Brien, or O'Keefe.   Or, harder still, some of the newer English of the birth of Ireland ; some planter of James the First's reign had annexed the estate of his late neighbour and friend ; nay, often his ally by marriage (and many another's estate besides) to his own already toowide domains, bent on making estated gentlemen of all his sons.

It was thus Broghill possessed himself of the manor of Blarney, and this many years before the army of Cromwell were assigned any lands for their arrears. After some wavering, he joined Cromwell upon his invasion of Ireland.   The Manor of Blarney seems to have been his price ; for, in every act and ordinance of Cromwell's Parliament there is always a proviso that nothing in the act contained should prejudice the right of Roger Lord Broghill to the Castle and Manor of

---

[1] " Autobiographical Preface to the History of my Historical Works and Theories," by Augustin Thierry.

Blarney. It was the ancestral seat of Donagh M'Carthy Viscount Muskerry, afterwards made Earl of Clancarty, married to Ormonde's eldest sister. It lay within seven miles of Cork, and Lord Muskerry and Broghill were neighbours and familiar friends. But Broghill had the thirst for Irish Confiscations like an hereditary disease inherent in his blood. He was son of that first Earl of Cork, who had come over to Ireland (as was commonly said) a bare-footed boy, not sixty years before, yet died the possessor of forfeited estates extending from the City of Cork eastward to Youghal, and northward to Lismore. Lord Broghill was not ashamed in his lust for land to possess himself of his friend Muskerry's noble castle and demesnes.

In like manner, Sir Charles Coote, first Earl of Mountrath, and son of the first settler of his name in Ireland, Provost Martial of Connaught, already largely rewarded by Queen Elizabeth and King James the First, with the richest pasture land in Roscommon, obtained through oppressive purchases from the wretched Connaught transplantaters, while he was the Chief Commissioner of the transplantation, some of these transplanters' lands at a shilling an acre, none higher than half a crown; and, amongst other purchases, the Castle and Demesne of Tyrellan, near the town of Galway, an ancient seat of the Marquis of Clanricarde.

It was to Tyrellan that he invited Colonel Sadleir, Governor of Galway, and his officers, to drink a cup of wine, in the year 1659. Leaving his guests there, under some excuse, he went by boat with Colonel Sadleir, to Galway, and induced him to order the gates to be opened. Sir Charles had a party there ready to

cry, " A Coote, a Coote," and, "a Free Parliament,"
the secret rallying cry of the Royalists. Sir Charles had
also Gormanston Castle. And for his greater conveni-
ence in attending the Council Board at Dublin Castle,
had a seven years' lease from Quarter-Master-General
Vernon, of Clontarf Castle. He was greatly disappointed on applying for it to Ormonde, to hear that
it had been given by the King to Colonel Ned Vernon,
the Quarter-Master-General's cousin, as great a darling
of the Royalists as the other was of Cromwell. Ormonde
apologised on the King's behalf, and regretted Sir
Charles had not spoken sooner. Sir Charles replied
in dudgeon, that he always feared what had happened,
that he "should be left in the suds," as he expressively, if
not elegantly, styled it, while attending his duty as
Lord Justice in Ireland.

Colonel Sir Theophilus Jones had Sarsfield's house
and demesne at Lucan. Both Sir Charles Coote and
Sir Theophilus Jones had been Commissioners for
trying and punishing any that should promote the
interest of Charles Stuart. But as has been said or
sung in Hudibras,

> " But when the times begin to alter,
> None rise so high as from an halter."

Sir Theophilus's brother, Dr. Henry Jones, Bishop
of Clogher, had Lynch's Knock, now known as
Summer Hill, near Trim. It adjoins Dangan, and
was in 1879, taken by the Empress of Austria as
a hunting seat. The Bishop had accepted the
Presbyterian Directory instead of the Book of Common
Prayer, and had in 1654, been a Commissioner to press
the engagement on the Presbyterians of Ulster to be
faithful to a government without a King or House of

Lords. At Carrickfergus he threatened the Earl or Clanbrassill and Viscount Montgomery of Ardes, on their refusing to take "the engagement" to be faithful to the Government as then established without King or House of Lords, with transplantation of themselves, families, and tenants to the County of Tipperary. For by Cromwell's Act for the settling of Ireland, Protestant royalists, if they had borne arms against the Parliament were to transplant no less than Irish Papists. But by an ordinance of 1654, Protestant Delinquents were at the discretion of the Council, to be allowed to compound, and the Earl of Clanbrassill and Viscount Montgomery compounded,—Clanbrassill for £9,000, and Montgomery for £3,000. But some were refused that favour. For, Sir James Shaen complained after the Restoration, that the Cromwellian Commissioners in setting forth lands to him for the purchases he had made to the extent of £6,500 of Transplanters' claims in Connaught, forced him to accept the estates of Sir George Bingham, Sir Edward Crofton, and others, "under the notion of Delinquent, uncompounding Protestants," to the extent of 165,000 acres. But by the advice of Orrery and others, "as well as out of his own loyal inclinations," he allowed these Protestants to enjoy their estates for three years before the Restoration.

Henry Cromwell had got Portumna Castle and Deer Park, on the Shannon, in the county of Galway, with 6,000 acres adjacent, as his inheritance. It was the ancient chief seat of the Marquis of Clanricarde. And the "Lord Harry" owned besides 8,000 acres of the finest land in Meath, and a like quantity in the neighbourhood of Nenagh, in the County of Tipperary,

set out to him for his own and his father's arrears.
Commissary General John Reynolds, Henry Cromwell's
brother-in-law, was granted Carrick Castle and Deer
Park, the earliest possession of the Earls of Ormonde
in Tipperary.   Kilcash, on the southern slope of
Slieve-na-mon, overlooking Carrick, Clonmel, and the
Valley of the Suir, the seat of Ormonde's younger
brother, Richard Butler, was in the hands of John
Blackwell, the younger, for a public debt due to his
father, part being for the cost of the scaffold for the
execution of King Charles the First.   Miles Corbett,
made Chief Baron in the Court of Exchequer in Ireland by Cromwell, and one of the Commissioners for
the government of Ireland, had got a lease of Malahide
Castle, the seat of the Talbots from the days of King
John.   He had sate in judgment on the King.   Colonel
Daniel Axtell was in possession of Ballyragget Castle,
in the County of Kilkenny, the principal mansion of
Viscounts   Mountgarret,   near   kinsmen   of   the
Ormondes.   Axtell commanded the guard of Halber-
tiers at the King's execution.

Most of these lands and mansions were soon restored
to their ancient owners.

Corbett and Axtell were executed as Regicides. Sir
Charles Coote restored Tyrellan at once to Clanricarde's successor.

Mr. Solicitor-General Reynolds, who had become
heir to his brother on his shipwreck in 1658, on the
Goodwin Sands, returning from the capture of Mar-
dyke, in Holland, hastened to meet Ormonde and
restore Carrick Castle and Deer Park.   And he afterwards reminded Ormonde how he had said at the
King's Mews, his then residence, what a pleasure it

was to deal with gentlemen, because of his keeping his deer park well paled and stocked.

Kilcash was only recovered from Blackwell for Colonel Richard Butler, with great difficulty, and by the accident that it had not been fully and legally and formally conveyed by Ormonde's grandfather, Sir Walter Butler, Earl of Ormonde, and thus the title descended to the Duke of Ormonde ; and by the Act of Settlement all Ormonde's lands were to be restored to him out of hand. He was thus enabled to oust Blackwell, and put back his brother Colonel Richard Butler, into Kilcash.

And here may be mentioned the history of the Irish estates of Oliver Cromwell, the Protector, and of Henry Cromwell, Lord Deputy of Ireland, under his father, and Lord Lieutenant under his brother, the shadowy and fugitive heir and successor of the Protector. Could it be conceived, unless on the evidence of authentic history, that the lands held in Ireland by Oliver Cromwell, and the Lord Harry his son, should be confirmed to them or to their families and the former owners left to starve ?

But the New Interested People, in other words the Cromwellians or the purchasers of Cromwellian Lots, with the policy of buying up or bribing all-powerful bodies, and of giving them an interest in supporting the Act of Settlement gave by that Act the lands lately held by the Regicides to the Duke of York. And lest the Duke should be awakened by the outcries of his unfortunate fellow soldiers, for he commanded a regiment of them in France and Flanders (writes one of his contemporaries), they gave him all the lands given to the Regicides as rewards for their iniquity ;

and by this contrivance lopped off the hand of His Royal Highness, which they might very well have hoped would be their sword and buckler too. And he gave not one foot of it to the old proprietors, though several concluded that he purposely got it to relieve those distressed soldiers that served under him in the Low Countries.[1]

The lands of many a poor Irish officer and soldier who had served for seven years in exile in Flanders under the Duke's own command, was included in the grant, but gratitude or pity never induced him to restore one.[2]

Oliver Cromwell had for his arrears as a soldier, several thousand acres of the finest land in the baronies of Ratoath and Dunboyne, in Meath, nearest to Dublin. On Oliver's death, his Meath lands passed to the Lord Harry, his son, and while the Lord Harry's own Tipperary lands in the North Riding, near Nenagh, were confirmed to himself, these Meath lands of Oliver's were by the Act of Settlement, secured to Sir William Russell, of Laugharne, in Carmarthenshire; while Henry Cromwell's Connaught lands on the belt of military planters, called the Mile Line, were by the same Act secured to John Russell, of Chippenham, in Cambridgeshire, closely connected with him by marriage.

And here it is fit to mark the wide difference

---

[1] Plunkett's History, M.S., C. P., lxiv., 189.

[2] Sir Hardress Waller alone, one of the Regicides, had the lands of 24 Irish families. "Here ensueth the names of the proprietors of the lands given to Sir Hardress Waller, in the county of Limerick: John Roch, of Limerick and Newcastle" (and so are they all named and listed). "Received from Lord Carlingford, October 23rd, 1663." Endorsement in Sir George Lane's hand, Secretary to the Duke of Ormonde, C. P., xviii., 361.

between the respective conditions of Henry Cromwell and his father, the Protector. Oliver was covered, it may truly be said, with King Charles's blood, as fully as the axe-man who flooded the scaffold with it. But Henry Cromwell was no Regicide,—nor was he excepted from pardon for his lands as he well might have been, and probably would have been, but for his humanity and courtesy to the Marchioness of Ormonde and other grandees of his own nation and religion. For there is no instance of his benefitting any of the Irish.

On the contrary, it was under his Lord Lieutenancy that Papists Convict were by Act of Parliament to forfeit two-thirds of their lands and goods in Connaught, *toties quoties*, unless they renounced the Pope's supremacy, the worship of the Virgin, and the Invocation of Saints at Quarter Sessions, when summoned for that purpose, reducing them to beggary, and contrary to all the fine promises of Cromwell that he meddled with no man's conscience, though he would not allow the celebration of the Mass. So that all the grand English praises of the Lord Harry's admirable Government of Ireland are mere falsehoods.

Henry Cromwell, not being excepted from pardon, became entitled under the scheme of the Convention of February, 1660, afterwards set forth in the King's Gracious Declaration for the Settlement of Ireland, to such of his lands as were set out for his arrears of service in Ireland as a soldier.

His Tipperary lands amounting to 6,400 acres Irish measure (10,363 English), he sold to Richard, Earl of Cork, and to Ormonde's son Richard, Earl of

Arran.[1]   Whether there was any private agreement for their influence and aid beforehand to be exerted in his favour does not appear, but is probable.  Of the 8,000 acres held by Henry Cromwell in Dunboyne and Ratoath Baronies in Meath, 5,000 acres were Oliver Cromwell's own arrears (to use the language of the Duke of York's agents), and these being secured by the Act of Settlement to Sir William Russell, of Laugharne, the Duke of York claimed 5,000 acres to be given him elsewhere.[2]  The remaining 3,000 acres Irish (equal to 4,858 English), were for the Lord Harry's own arrears (amongst them poor Luke Sedgrave's lands of Killeglan).   These Henry Cromwell sold to Sir William Russell, of Laugharne,[3] an uncle of his wife's, and they were subsequently secured to Sir William Russell, by the Act of Settlement in the joint names of himself and Dr. Jonathan Goddard, a trustee for Sir William Petty.[4]

Meanwhile, the former inhabitants during the rule of the Commonwealth, were either pining in confinement and misery in Connaught, or, as soldiers of Charles the Second, had taken conditions from the King of Spain. The nobility and higher gentry, who had been colonels,

---

[1] Abstract of Grants under the Acts of Settlement and Explanation. Record Commissioners' Report.  Vol. iii.  Folio size, Printed.

[2] An Abstract of the Regicides' Names, and the number of acres of their lands within the several counties in Ireland claimed by Robert Gorges in behalf of His Royal Highness, and Controverted.  Clarendon papers, unbound, Bodleian Library, Oxford.  And see the paper in full in the Final Report on the Carte Papers, by C. W. Russell, D.D., and John P. Prendergast, 8vo, 1871.  Eyre and Spottiswood, pp. 170-180.

[3] Sir William Russell, of Chippenham, in Cambridgeshire.  The first Baronet had two sons named William.  The first, known as the Black Sir William, called "The Cream of the Russell's," for his loyalty ; the second, after the Black Sir William's death, born of his father's third wife, called ' The White Sir William, or Sir William of Laugharne."  He was made a baronet in 1660.  See Sir Bernard Burke's Extinct Baronetage.

[4] Section ccxviii.

lieutenant-colonels, and captains of the army commissioned by the king in Ireland in the years 1649, and
who fought against Cromwell and Ireton, till 1652,
obtained similar rank in the regiments formed abroad,
out of the 40,000 men, and more, that had retired to
Spain and Flanders between 1652 and 1655.

Military service abroad was the resource of all the
gentry, except those who were too old or weak to fly,
or were detained by a charge of family and children,
and were without means to maintain them in foreign
countries. The Duke of York, the Duke of Gloucester, the Marquis of Ormonde, Lord Muskerry,
became colonels-in-chief, the principal exiled landed
proprietors lieutenant-colonels and commissioned
officers ; the lesser gentry, non-commissioned officers.
Many a gentleman even trailed a pike as a common
soldier among his former tenants and followers,
happy thus to find a living that brought no disgrace or
forfeiture of social rank. The Irish regiments abroad
deemed themselves, during all the period of their service, subjects of King Charles the Second. They
marched and fought under his standards or ensigns,
and (unfortunately for themselves) held his commands
paramount.

This is what the king himself says of them in his
Gracious Declaration of the 30th November, 1660,
for the Settlement of Ireland (afterwards embodied in
the Act of Settlement).[1] In fact, they changed sides

---

[1] "We did, and must always remember the great affection a considerable
portion of this Nation exprest to us during the time of our being beyond
the Seas, when, with all cheerfulness and obedience, they received and sub-
mitted to our orders, and betook themselves to that service which we
directed as most convenient and behoofeful at that time to us, though
attended with inconvenience enough to themselves."—14 & 15 Chas. II.,
chap. 2, clause 4.

according to his wishes, from Spain to France, and from France to Spain, making him powerful abroad by having such a force at his back.   They had their return to Ireland constantly in view.   They fought and bled to establish a claim to be restored.   Their hopes, accordingly, at the Restoration, were high.   They had dissolved their Confederation in 1648, and put their forces under the king's command, represented by Ormonde.   They were promised by the Peace of 1648, an Act of Pardon and Oblivion and restoration to their estates.   They had proclaimed him king in Ireland, and fought against Cromwell to recover his crown for him, and had laid him under fresh obligations by their services beyond sea.   Both obligations were acknowledged by the King's Declaration for the Settlement of Ireland.

CHAPTER II.

THE CROMWELLIANS RECALL THE KING ON CONDITION
OF SECURING THEM THEIR LANDS.

THE Cromwellian grandees were skilful enough to secure
the possessions they had obtained from the Parliament
or from grants of Cromwell. Sir Charles Coote,
Lord Broghill, Sir Theophilus Jones, and others
presaging the ruin that would fall upon the Cromwellian system by Cromwell's death in September,
1658, got possession in December, 1659, of the Castle
of Dublin, and in February, 1660, summoned
representatives of counties and boroughs on the old
system to meet as a Convention of Estates at the Four
Courts, Dublin, then held in buildings attached to
Christ Church. Sir Charles Coote sent over
Lord Forbes to Bruges to tell the King he was, for his
own part, able and ready to restore him at once. His
conditions were, that he should keep all the lands he
had got, from the Parliament, from Cromwell, or as a
purchaser of Transplanters' lots in Connaught, and the
same terms to such friends as he should name, as
assisting him. To all which the King agreed. But
it was arranged that the motions of General Monck
should be waited for. Agents came to the King from
Monck to Breda, and on the 14th of April, 1660, there
was issued the King's letter from Breda, promising the
Adventurers and soldiers their possessions, and the
Connaught purchasers their acquisition. This was to
've (as Sir Maurice Eustace wrote to Ormonde) the
ates of those that had fought for him, to those that

had fought against him. Eustace was shocked at the projected iniquity. On the 30th of November, 1660, there issued the King's Gracious Declaration for the Settlement of Ireland and all interests there, and six and thirty Commissioners were named to execute it. The English, by the King's Declaration, were to keep nearly all they had got, the Irish to be restored to nearly all they had lost. This was a juggle. It was too early, too soon after the services rendered by the Irish officers and soldiers to throw them over openly. Accordingly, it was pretended that there would be an immense fund for reprising such Cromwellians as should be put out for King's friends, by the estates of fanatics and regicides, by forged debentures and false admeasurements. And the fund would be increased by the lands of Nunciotists, and such Irish as had rejected the Peaces of 1646 and 1648. It was only on 20th March, 1661, that the 36 Commissioners opened their Court ; but as they were all in possession of lands taken from the Irish, the Irish claimants deemed it useless to plead before such interested judges. The Commissioners were further unfitted to be judges by their want of training, and by their numbers. So negligent were they of the claims of the weak, that after several months' sitting they had not restored above one widow, " though our streets (as Lord Chancellor, Sir Maurice Eustace, wrote to Ormonde), be full of those miserable creatures of all sorts, noble as well as of inferior degree." [1]

The Commissioners seemed more busy in selecting residences for themselves from amongst the deserted houses of the Irish in Dublin. " Their partiality and

[1] Eustace to Ormonde, August 21, 1661.  C. P. xxxi., 167.

corruption," to use the language of the King, "had discredited the Declaration itself."[1]

Their Court was virtually closed in April, 1662, and five new Commissioners were sent over to administer the Act of Settlement passed on 27th September, 1662.

Imagination then may easily paint the scene that Ireland presented at the opening of this Second Court of Claims.

Round the doors of the newly opened Court may be pictured an anxious crowd of impoverished noblemen, and tattered gentlemen of old descent, some of English blood, some of pure Irish, many of them soldiers of foreign air, "With patched buff coats, jack boots and Bilboa blade," broken-hearted widows and orphans. These were the Irish. Some of these officers had spent six years in misery in Connaught; some, ten years in sieges and battles under perpetual fire in France, Italy and Flanders. For, from the known bravery of their race, they were ever allowed the post of honour, while it happened also to be the post of danger:[2] Others had dwelt in garrets and cellars at Paris or Bruges.

By the King's Declaration of 30th November, 1660, embodied in the Act of Settlement, the restorable Irish were of four classes,—Innocents ; Ensignmen, as those were styled, who had rallied to the King's Ensigns abroad ; Article men, or those promised pardon and restoration by the Articles of the Peace made between Ormonde on the King's behalf and Confederate

---

[1] King's Letter, February, 1663. C. P. xliii., 64.
[2] Sir Charles Wogan to Dean Swift, February 27th, 1734. Swift's "Works," edited by Sir Walter Scott, vol. xvii., 449.

B

Catholics in 1648 ; and the King's Nominees, thirty-
six Irish noblemen and gentlemen, named in the
Declaration, to be restored without further proof by
the special favour of the King.    To these Nominees
were added the "Thirty-six sufferers from the
violence of the Nuncio." Innocents were to be
re-invested with their lands and houses at once, and
the Cromwellians thus removed to be reprised, that
is, to get in return, as good lands as they gave up.
Widows, men that were boys at school in 1641, or
abroad studying in France, Spain, or the Low Countries,
lunatics at the outbreak in 1641, or aged, sick,
impotent, and (to use the language of the Act), " such
as had been transplanted merely for their religion,"
were among the Innocents.

But if any of them had lived at his home in Munster
or Connaught, or in the parts under the rule of the
Confederates, though never so quietly, it was a bar to
innocence.    This was to "have lived in the Irish
quarters ;" and yet no English garrison would trust
them, nor had food for them.    If it was alleged in
their behalf, that the law never before had deemed
the family criminal that lived quietly in their own
home, doing nothing (as Sir Nicholas Plunket urged
before the King and Council at Whitehall), it was
answered by Sir Charles Coote : " If this disqualifi-
cation be taken off, the number of Innocents will be
so great, that it will endanger the interests of the
Adventurers and Soldiers ; and will give the Irish a
majority in Parliament." And if the Innocent had
accepted land in Connaught, he was " postponed,"
which was equivalent to being dismissed, although he
and his family were driven thither, and would be

hanged, or else transported, if they stayed ; or starved unless they took the pittance of land offered for their support. In order, then, to be restored, they must claim in default of Innocency, as Article men, under the Articles of the Peace of 1648. This promised to the Irish, who observed it, a pardon and restoration. The claimant would then be called " an Article man." But Article men were only to be restored after Innocents had been provided for. If he could not claim articles, he must then resort to his claim as Ensignman, one of those "who continued with and served faithfully under our Ensigns beyond the seas." These, however, though the best deserving, were to be restored last of all.

Ellen, Viscountess Dowager of Ikerrin, claimed as an Innocent. With her deceased Lord, she had been transplanted from Lismalin Park, near Roscrea, in the county of Tipperary, to Connaught. Her husband's misery in 1656, had extorted the pity of His Highness the Lord Protector, who wrote to the Lord Deputy Fleetwood, his son-in-law, that Lord Ikerrin should not be allowed to perish for want of subsistence.[1] Lord Ikerrin was at rest in 1662, but his Nocency, if any could have been proved, would not affect the Lady Ikerrin his wife. It was only Cromwellian justice that could inflict penalty on a wife for her husband's acts. She was decreed Innocent.

The Lady Dunboyne, widow of Piers, Lord Dunboyne, was less fortunate. The Butlers of Kiltinan, a branch of the house of Ormonde, were ennobled as Lords Dunboyne by King Henry the Eighth. For

---

[1] Cromwellian Settlement of Ireland, second Edition, p. 180.  Gill, Dublin, Thomas Wyee, 1875.

ages they had dwelt at Kiltinan Castle, near Fethard, in the county of Tipperary. It was from Kiltinan that Lord and Lady Dunboyne were transplanted to Connaught in 1655, with their twenty tenants, and their respective stocks of cows, sheep, garrons and swine.[1] Kiltinan Castle stands at the edge of a perpendicular cliff ninety feet deep in the rere. A gushing river breaks forth from the rock below, on the level of the ground, and there joins the river Anner, and steps are cut in the cliff, with a stone-work covering for the garrison to draw water in safety.

Who that has seen this lordly castle, but has pictured to himself the departure of these exiles to Connaught, from the place where the Lords Dunboyne had dwelt for 400 years ; lands that Piers Lord Dunboyne had sported over as a youth, and had titled as a man,—whither he had brought his bride, and there with its mother had fondled their first-born and only child, a daughter, and had hoped to spend long years of happiness ?

At the King's restoration, she returned from Connaught, but her husband was dead, the time for claiming Innocence was past, and the estate was held by an Adventurer. Lady Dunboyne had only by the charity of the Duchess of Ormonde, a mountain farm, at five shillings a year, on the slope of Slieve-na-mon, in sight of her former abode, to live on ; as without it, she must have died.

After the issuing of the King's Declaration, a set of Instructions were forwarded to the Commissioners for their guidance in executing the Declaration, containing eleven bars to Innocence. It was hoped few

[1] Ibid., p. 23.

would be able to pass them. Among the bars was one, that no one should prove his claim through a Nocent father. But they forgot that where a father was tenant for life, with an estate to his eldest son in remainder, the law held that the son did not claim through the father. Another bar was to have dwelt before the Cessation of Arms or Truce of September 1643 in the rebel quarters.

Thomas Wyse, son of Andrew Wyse of Dungarvan, deceased, claimed as son and heir of an Innocent. His father was so palsied as to be unable to feed himself, and being stripped of all his goods by the English and Irish in turn, he removed from his dwelling near Dungarvan into Waterford, to a friend's house, where he died in September, 1642. But Waterford in 1642 was Irish quarters, and it was contended that this made his father Nocent, and that therefore the claim was barred. But the claimant proved that his father was tenant for life, and that his own estate was in remainder, and therefore that he did not claim through his father. And his claim was allowed.[1] Lunatics could not, of course, be deemed criminal.

David Howlin was proved to be distracted, and could not speak a word of sense; he was, in a manner, an idiot for seven years before the war, and he continued so to the day of his claim. He would run away some· times a week together, and eat grass. Nothing being objected to him, he was decreed Innocent.[2]

Another claimant of Innocence was John Lattin, a Lunatic, but with lucid intervals.

[1] Sir Edward Deering's Minutes of Decrees in the Court of Claims. C. P. lxvii.
[2] C. P.

John Lattin, of Morristown, in the county of Kildare, was distracted in his mind before 1641. But in his lucid intervals he always exclaimed against the plunderings and outrages done on the Protestants. He and his heavy charge of eight children were accordingly spared from transplantation to Connaught, but his lands were forfeited for being a Papist and for being unable to prove his Constant Good Affection. Stephen Lattin, his son, presented his case to the King at the Restoration. Stephen had served three years in the King's army in foreign parts, as a common soldier in the Duke of York's regiment. The King, by Letter under Privy Seal, adjudged John Lattin Innocent within the meaning of the term in the King's Gracious Declaration for the Settlement of Ireland of 30th November, and accordingly ordered him to be forthwith restored as well to his houses in Naas, and his lands of Morristown, as also to such other lands as he or his cousin Alison Lattin were seized of, the present possessors to be forthwith reprised.[1]

Though the taking of land in Connaught was not included among the bars to Innocence, but only caused the claimant to be "postponed," it virtually became a bar. For, the time for hearing more than 7,500 claims of Innocence was only seven months. Not one-sixth had been heard when the time was expired. And when the Court opened again in January, 1666, it was only a Court for Protestants and English—the hearing of all further claims of Innocence by Papists was barred.

[1] Privy Seal dated February 26th, 1661.

Luke Sedgrave was one of the disappointed Innocents, through the want of time to hear him. Three years before the rebellion, Luke Sedgrave of Killeglan, 7 miles north of Dublin, near Ratoath, was sent for his education to the Low Countries, but was called home by his parents through their want of means.

At Killeglan he always maintained an English garrison until he was turned out by the late usurpers, and transplanted to Connaught, but took no lands there. Luke Sedgrave's claim of Innocence, as he set forth in his Petition, was not heard through the shortness of the time. His civility and loyalty was attested by Sir Thomas Harman, Captain of Ormonde's Life Guard, who was quartered at Killeglan during the war. Killeglan had been set out to Henry Cromwell for his arrears. French, Bishop of Ferns, had heard that the Duchess of Ormonde had on her knees obtained from the King that Harry Cromwell should keep all his lands set out for his arrears, in return for his kindness to her and her family, during Oliver's reign. Luke Sedgrave being dead in 1675, his widow, Miss Jane Nottingham, " a virtuous woman of a constantly loyal family," said the Bishop of Ferns, " wandered with her children in poverty without jointure or relief."

Another postponed Innocent was John Cheevers.

John Cheevers of Grangefort, county of Carlow, was of the house of Cheevers of Maystown, in Meath. They had, as he said, lands given them by King Henry the Second at the Conquest. He fled with his family to Dublin, at the outbreak of 1641, and took lodgings for a year with Mrs. Alison Ashe of Kilmainham, near Dublin, but was forced back to the country by the Lords Justices Proclamation against Popish

strangers. He and his family were in 1654 transplanted to Connaught. And for taking a pittance of
land there to keep them from starving, he was postponed in the first Court of Claims ; and when the
Commissioners sat again in the second Court, in January, 1666, to administer the Act of Explanation, all
claims of Innocence were foreclosed.[1]

Sir Patrick Barnewall's father and family, with Sir
Patrick himself, were transplanted, and his father was
allotted lands there, for the ancestral estate he was
removed from in Meath. He was only tenant for life.
But Sir Patrick having joined him in selling 40 acres
of his Connaught allotment, at the request of the purchaser, this was held as an admission by way of
estoppel, that he had accepted lands, and he was postponed, though his father was obliged to give up his
Connaught assignment to the Earl of Clanricarde, and
thus Sir Patrick lost his estate of £2,000 a year in
Meath, for all farther claims of Innocence were barred
by the new Act, and thus he had neither lands in
Connaught nor elsewhere.

The acceptance of land in Connaught was alleged to
be the transplanter's own act. But an Irish pam-
phleteer of the day ridicules the term "Postponed
Innocents," for if a man did not go to Connaught he
would be hanged, and unless he took land there, as Sir
Nicholas Plunket said, he and his family must be
starved. And he then continues : "If a man condemned to die go on hands and feet to the gallows, is
he therefore to be concluded Felo de se ? Oh, Jack !
Our brethren over-act their parts, and, Nero-like, in

---

[1] Liber M. Collections relating to the Act of Settlement. State Paper
Office, Dublin Castle.

their Capitols, sit and rejoice at their fellow-subjects' destruction."[1]

The case of Elizabeth, widow of Captain Henry Rochfort, granddaughter of General Thomas Preston, first Viscount Tara, is a sad one, and shows the difficulty an Irish Innocent had of recovering her rights even under a decree of innocence, though never so powerfully friended.

These Rochforts were old English. They had furnished Justiciaries and Lords Deputy. One branch having become Protestant, were, in later times, made Earls of Belvedere. General Thomas Preston, second son of Christopher Preston, Viscount Gormanston, came over from the Low Countries in 1642 to offer his sword and the skill he had acquired in the Spanish service to his countrymen, and served as General of the Confederate Catholic forces for Leinster until he retired in 1651 to France on the decline of their power, and died there in 1654. In 1650 he was created Viscount Tara, and left a son Anthony,— second Viscount, married to Margaret Warren, entitled to an estate in the King's County, daughter of Anthony Warren ; and by her had children, amongst others Elizabeth, the wife of Captain Rochfort, named among the Ensignmen.

Anthony, Viscount Tara and the Viscountess both died, and the orphan children were left to the care of Miss Warren, their Aunt. The King was under great obligations to the family, and wrote to the Earl of Orrery, one of the Lords Justices, a letter with his own hand. " My Lord Orrery (said the King), when

[1] Inspection into the Lapsed Money and other things. (A.D. 1666). C.P. lix. 228.

I came first to Bruges, in Flanders, and was far from being in a good condition, I found my Lord Tara there, who invited me to his house, where I lodged near a month . . . . and during the whole of my abode in those parts, he gave me frequent evidence of his good affection, which I resolved to have requited if he had lived, and therefore since he and his wife are dead, I must particularly recommend his children to you, and likewise their Aunt, Miss Warren, who was there likewise . . . . that they may be out of hand put into possession of the several lands which belong to them."[1]

But the Adventurers and Soldiers in possession refused.

Meantime Miss Warren and the orphans were ordered a pension. But it was often in arrear ; and in 1682 Ormonde wrote to his son, the Earl of Arran, Lord Deputy, he hoped it would be paid in consideration of the reception Miss Warren "gave the King and all of us at Bruges, in her sister's house."[2]

It is not surprising that the Adventurers and Soldiers refused possession. They were secured by the King's Declaration for the Settlement. And the young Lord Tara, whose father and grandfather had borne high military rank amongst the Irish, could not claim as an Innocent through either of them, because of their Nocency. He never regained his estate.

But Elizabeth's husband, Captain Henry Rochfort, was different. He had served the King abroad. Elizabeth Preston had not long been married to him,

---

[1] Dated "Whitehall, 4th August, 1662." Endorsed "Coppie of a Letter writt by the King's Owne hande." C. P. xlii. 191.

[2] Ormonde to Arran from London, 26th September, 1682. Ibid. ccxix. 289.

when she was left an afflicted widow, pregnant. Captain Henry Rochfort, of Kilbride, in Meath, was son of
Robert, and his mother was Ellinor Fleming, one of
the sisters of Lord Slane. By a marriage settlement
of 1639 large estates in Meath had been settled on
him in remainder. At the age of 15 he served under
Ormonde as Ensign in the Earl of Carlingford's
regiment at the defeat of Rathmines in 1649. And
when the Usurped Power became prevalent he went
over seas, and enlisted himself under his Majesty's
Ensigns. On 31st August, 1663, he obtained a Decree of Innocence, and to be restored to all his estate
except what lay in the suburbs of Kells and Trim, and
for these a reprise in the neighbourhood out of forfeited lands undisposed of.

Some of the lands being withheld, his widow besought the King for a letter to Ormonde, Lord Lieutenant ; and, the better to move his Majesty's pity,
urged her request not only on her own behalf, but on
that of the unborn infant she carried in her womb.[1]

But these Decrees of Innocence infuriated the
Cromwellians. In many a castle was some fierce
Colonel, Captain, or man at arms determined to maintain by the sword (if he could not do it by chicane),
what he had gained by the sword. Thus Lord Masse-
reene said of the Debate in the House of Peers
touching Sir Henry O'Neill's estate in his possession,
taking at length the King's printed Declaration in his
hand, " That he would have the benefit of it by this,"
putting his other hand to his sword. For the King
ordered Sir Henry O'Neill to be restored to Kil-
lileagh, Co. Antrim, though not named in the Declara-

[1] C. P. xliii. 225.

†

tion, and though he had resided with his mother (being then however only 14) in the rebels' quarters, and had taken lands in Connaught, all bars to restora- tion.[1] Or like Colonel Edward Warren, who com- manded one of Axtell's regiments, that told one Mr. Birmingham, seeking to recover as an Innocent, some lands in his possession by right of an entail—" If the English again take arms in their hands, they will cut off your ' tayles.' " Or, like Serjeant Beverley, at Kilbeggan, in the King's County, who, having heard that he was called " one of Cromwell's doggs," answered that they should let Cromwell alone, for he was the best man that ever reigned in the three nations, or that ever would ; and if the King thought to take away their lands that they had gained by Cromwell and their swords, he should be deceived, " for they would have one knock for it first, his (Beverley's) life for it."

Their discontent was evidenced by more than words.

The Lady Anne, widow of the Marquis of Clan- ricarde, being restored, by order of the Lords Justices, to her only jointure-house in Ireland, the Castle and Bawn of Kilcolgan, five soldiers, under the command of Captain Brice of the garrison of Galway, on the night of the 7th August, 1662, got over the wall of the Bawn, and burst into a house where two of the servants slept in charge of the Castle for the Mar- chioness, and drove them out, and carried away the doors, and broke the angles, making it uninhabitable, and forcibly detained it, in contempt of the Order in Council.[2]

---

[1] 6th March, 1660-1. C. P. xli. 177.
[2] C. P. lx. 230.

A more signal violence was committed on Lady Susan Taaffe.

On Sunday morning the 29th of October, 1663, as appeared by the petition of Christopher Taaffe and Lady Susan his wife, Captain John Chambers and a band under his orders, in the absence of her husband, broke into the house of Tullikeely, in the County of Louth, held by her husband under his kinsman, Theobald Taaffe, Earl of Carlingford, and finding her and her daughter there, violently laid hands upon her, and by force took her in a blanket, and laid her on a dunghill, and threw her daughter down stairs, so that she fainted, and was so bruised that she was still on 10th December following, in danger of her life. And all this barbarous usage and insolence was done, said Lady Susan, by Captain Chambers in behalf of his brother Parson Chambers, contesting the Earl of Carlingford's title to Ballikeely,—Parson Chambers, she added, being one of the persons who was named in the Proclamation, and had fled for the phanatick plot.[1]

Similar violence exhibited in Doctor William Petty's behalf, caused the death of the eldest son and heir of Patrick Moore, of Downstown, in Meath. This young man's father and grandfather had shed their blood both in Ireland, France, and Flanders, in the King's service. The first in the capacity of Secretary of State in Holland, was able to obtain money for the King's necessities, and got run through the thigh in defending it from capture by an Irish faction. He risked his life in bringing intelligence of the state of England to the

---

[1] C.P., clix. 83.

King in his exile at the Hague. Both father and son served under the King's Ensigns abroad, and the father nearly lost his life for bringing away Sir James Darcy's regiment from the King of France's service, to the King's in Holland, and they were thus despoiled and disappointed Ensignmen. And the son was further a disappointed Innocent, shut out by the shortness of time for hearing Innocents. The case is thus an instance at once of the loyalty, and the services and sufferings of so many Irish families.

Patrick Moore, before the rebellion of 1641, was possessed of Dowanestown (now called Downstown), in Meath, near Duleek, besides other lands in the counties of Dublin, Kildare, Meath, and Louth, as well as of houses and lands in the Corporations of Drogheda and Dundalk. These he settled on his eldest son of the same name, in 1637. In that year his son went to England to study the law, and there continued until he was driven thence in the year 1643, into Flanders, Holland, and other parts of the Low Countries for his loyalty and religion.

His father rallied to the King's Ensigns in France, and was an officer in the Duke of York's regiment, and when His Majesty left France for Flanders, by Cardinal Mazarin's orders, Patrick Moore stole away most part of Sir James Darcy's regiment, being Moore's cousin-german, for the King's service, and would have been murdered for it by Sir James Darcy, only that he got notice of it. Patrick Moore then became one of the Secretaries of State in Holland, and obtained several sums of money for the King, which his son, the petitioner believed, Ormonde might remember ; at all events, Father Peter Walsh would, as he came with

Moore's father to give Ormonde an account of it:
While bringing this money to the King, his father was
set upon by Colonel Fitzmorris, who would fain have
persuaded his father to give him the money for the
Irish faction then in Spain, but his father refusing,
Colonel Fitzmorris and several others, lay in wait for
him, and would have killed him, only for the Countess
of Arundel's cries, none being by but the Countess,
and he was thus saved, though run through the thigh.
During the time that the King kept his Court at the
Hague, his father, then one of the Secretaries of State
in Holland, was at different times authorised to go into
England on the Countess of Arundel's affairs, and
always brought back news of the state of affairs there
to the King, to his (Moore's) great risk.   And for this
his son refers to Sir Edward Walker, Garter King of
Arms, or Father Peter Walsh, better than the
petitioner could remember, being then but young.
Besides this, his father after the King's Restoration,
subscribed the Royal Remonstrance (or Catholic
Declaration of Loyalty), and publicly defended the
Remonstrance which " got his said father a great
deal of anger amongst the gentry and clergy."

Soon after the Restoration, his father died, and
petitioner's title having accrued, the petitioner's eldest
son got into possession of Dowanestown, the petitioner's
Mansion House, which had been obtained in the
Usurper's time by Dr. William Petty, " under some
surreptitious Injunction against all laws." But Dr.
Petty had him dragged out and left in the open air,
his son being then in a burning fever.   And of this
hardship, his son suddenly died.   The petitioner however got back into possession by connivance (as he

candidly admitted), of Doctor Petty's tenant.  But the Doctor having obtained an Injunction from the Commissioners of Claims to be restored unless cause to the contrary were shown in ten days.  Patrick Moore petitioned Ormonde for his aid.  But he must have failed of his purpose ; for, by a subsequent petition, he besought Ormonde to have him enlisted (*i.e.* placed on the list), in His Majesty's Gracious Establishment.[1]

This unfortunate Mr. Patrick Moore was another Innocent debarred of his hearing for want of time.  For being in England in duress (*i.e.* imprisoned as an Irish Papist), at the time of the sitting of the Court of Claims, he got His Majesty's order for a hearing after the lapsing of his time, and if found innocent, to be restored to all his estate as well within Corporations as without.  But he never obtained the benefit of it, though he sent over his Majesty's Letter under Privy Seal.  And thus lost both his eldest son, and his ancestral estate.[2]

Sir Audley Mervyn, Speaker of the House of Commons, set Adventurers and Soldiers in a flame by his celebrated "Puckan[3] Speech."  He moved in the Commons House a set of new and stricter rules for the Commissioners of the Court of Claims in judging of Innocence.

In addition, he suggested that the title deeds of those who had failed to prove their Innocence, should be taken away from them.  "It could not work them a prejudice," said he, "for the lands being adjudged from them, what purpose can the writings serve in their hands ?"

[1] C. P. lx. 106.  Ibid. 125.
[2] Ibid.
[3] Puckan is the Irish for goat.  It was applied also to the stuffed calf described here.

" But Sir (he continued), I correct myself. They will have an operation. And this puts me in mind of a plain but apposite similitude. Sir, in the North of Ireland, the Irish have a custom in winter when the milk is scarce, to kill the calf, and reserve the skin, and stuffing it with straw, they set it upon four wooden legs, and the cow will be as fond of it as she was of the living calf; she will low after it, and lick it, and give her milk down, so it stands but by her.

" These writing wanting the land, are but skins stuffed with straw; but Sir, they will low after them, lick them over in their thoughts, teach their children to read out of them, instead of horn books, and if any venom be left, they will give it down upon the sight of these writings, and entail a memory of revenge, though the Estate Tail be cut off."

The House of Commons adopted the new rules for the Court of Claims, and to render their concurrence the more impressive, accompanied Sir Audley, their Speaker, through the streets to the Presence Chamber in the Castle, to deliver the suggested rules to the Duke of Ormonde. They virtually charged the Commissioners with High Treason (said the King in his Letter reproving the House), as having a design to destroy the English Protestant interest in Ireland. The speech was printed and distributed in thousands over the country. A plot was formed by Col. Alexander Jephson and other Cromwellians to seize the Duke of Ormonde and the Castle of Dublin, then the magazine of gunpowder and arms, to restore religion according to the Covenant, and that the English should possess such lands as they had under Cromwell, and to abolish the Court of Claims then, as they alleged, ruining the

c

country. But the Duke of Ormonde got notice of Jephson's arrival in Dublin,—had him arrested,—and Colonel Jephson, Colonel Edward Warren, and one Thompson, were tried, convicted, and on the 13th of July, 1663, were hanged, and their heads set up at Dublin Castle. By this self-sacrifice, they saved the Cromwellian Interest. For in the following month, on 21st of August, 1663, the Court of Irish Innocents (as it might well be styled) closed, and remained so till the 4th of January, 1666, when it was opened again as a Court for English and Protestants only, or for such Irish as had provisoes in the Act of Explanation ordering them restoration without the incumbrance of a previous reprisal.

By the Act of Settlement the time for hearing Claims of Innocence was limited to one year, from the opening of the Court. The Commissioners opened this Court by reading their Commission on the 20th of September, 1662 ; but the preparing of rules and other formalities hindered them from hearing of Claims until on the 13th of January, 1663. And as the year of Twelve Lunar months closed on the 21st of August, 1663, they had little more than six months for hearing of over seven thousand claims. As the time of closing drew near, the poorer and weaker claimants piteously besought the Commissioners for a hearing. Ladies and orphans who had been in the lists for hearing, found that they had been superseded by more powerful persons, and prayed for some certain day to be set for their trial. They were almost consumed, they said, with long attendance without subsistence in that city as well as their helpless families in the country, and their Honours were designed by God and the King for relief of the oppressed widows and orphans such as the petitioners were.[1]

There was some correspondence by Ormonde and others, about extending the time for hearing. Ormonde said " the time must be extended let it trouble whom it might." And Orrery, assuming a tone of virtue and humanity far from his real character, said that if the time limited was not enough (as he expected) he would when it was expired be most forward to get it extended. " For God forbid," said he " any Innocent should be precluded for want of time to hear him ;" adding, " If any Englishman, were he my brother or my son desired one foot of an Irishman's lands that shall be found Innocent, I wish he might be buried in it ; and from my soul I declare, if Ireland should be settled on any foundations but those of justice, I think it will never prosper, but moulder to nothing."[2]

Yet it was this very Orrery that framed the Act of Explanation[3] that shut the doors of the new Court of Claims against six thousand unheard Irish and upwards, who had filed their claims of Innocence.

Such, for instance, was the case of Joan Archer, otherwise Bourke, widow of Captain Thomas Archer, of Corbettstown, in County of Kilkenny, and Mary Archer, her daughter. The Archers of Corbettstown were an

---

[1] Liber C. 248. Signed, Alice Browne alias Plunket, her son Mathew Nangle, Isaac Purcell, Pierce Nangle, Al. Chesley, Thomas Geoghegan, Eliz. Dalton, Margt. Dalton, alias Lince, widow and her five orphans ; Margt. Tyrrell, widow, John Nangle and Elizth. his mother, Mary Plunkett alias Nangle, John Malden alias Dalton, Geoghegan Marks, May Purcell, Wm. Nangle, Oliver Uniell, Geo. Walsh, Mary Fox alias FitzGerald, and Con and Hugh Fox, orphans ; James Linham alias Moore, Mary Linham alias Moore, Edmond Walsh, Ibid.

[2] Orrery to Clarendon, Dublin, 12th March, 1663.

[3] Passed 23rd December, 1665.

ancient and respectable family well known to Ormonde. Her husband, Captain Thomas Archer, was slain under Ormonde's command at the siege of Drogheda by Cromwell in August, 1649. Since the loss of Captain Archer, said his widow, she and her daughter had remained in a miserable and starving condition, like poor pilgrims wandering from place to place, having been unable by the dissolution of the Court of Claims to get their claim to the estate descended to them after the death of Captain Archer, heard.[1]

Who can tell what numbers wandered about as beggars, near their once happy homes—or died broken-hearted—or perished through want ?[2] The father (said a contemporary writer) is not able to help the child, nor the child the father. Mothers are weeping over their little ones, languishing in want and hunger,[3] and many widows and orphans are perishing of want in the view of the world by that fatal sentence called the Bill of Settlement.[4] Other distressed widows and minors were crying out for justice and not heard—poor, desolate, and dejected, they were waiting at the door of the palace, and no regard was had of their prayers and petitions.[5]

Another, writing a few years later, speaks of the extinction of so many hundred illustrious families, and the pitiful groans of surviving heirs, and the repentant sobs of their dying fathers for having brought

---

[1] Petition, 20th March, 1664. C. P. clix. 178.
[2] Plunket's History, p. 1128. C. P. lxiv.
[3] Preface to Clarendon's Settlement and Sale of Ireland, printed at Louvain, 1668, p. 59. Duffy's Edition. 12mo. Dublin, 1846.
[4] Ibid., p. 53.
[5] Ibid., p. 18.

them, by entering into rebellion, to misery and ruin.[1]

To pass from Innocents to Ensignmen.

There were two hundred and twenty-three named in the Declaration ; but there was a crowd of others constantly petitioning to be added to the list, as having been forgotten because of absence.

Upon the King's return, the Ensignmen were, for the first year or so, more fortunate than some others of their countrymen. Little did they then expect that not one of them would get, by the King's Declaration or Acts of Settlement, so much of their fathers' lands as would serve for a grave.[2]

For by the provisions of the Act of Settlement the Cromwellian in possession must be first reprised before the Ensignman, the former owner, could be restored, and there were no reprisals to be had.

An order for restoration was consequently well likened to a rattle given to a starving child crying for bread.[3]

And it was said with truth that all these gentlemen were rendered ridiculous, and their names put in print only to be laughed at.[4]

At the reduction of Ireland in 1662 Cromwell was in amity with Spain, and thousands of Irish Officers

---

[1] Loyal Remonstrance, by Father Peter Walsh. Preface IV. Folio. London. 1673.

[2] Sec. 1124. " The Irish that was abroad followed the King in the French and Spanish services, as well they of the Nuncio's party as the Ormondists. Not one of them got by the Act of Settlement as much land as would serve for a grave." Collections by friends, some of them eye-witnesses, being a Treatise or Account of the Warr or Rebellion in Ireland since the year 1641.—Carte Papers, vol. 64, pp. 418, 431. MS.

[3] Plunket's History, p. 1134.

[4] Ibid. See also Clauses xxv. and xxvi. of the Declaration of Settlement.

and their men, with Cromwell's consent, took conditions with the King of Spain. From the time of Queen Elizabeth, when Stanley, an English Catholic, in command of an Irish regiment sent over by Queen Elizabeth to aid the revolted Hollanders against the Spaniards, carried over his regiment to the Spanish service, the Irish had always been confided in by the Kings of Spain. They had on all occasions the right hand, and were particularly called by the name of brothers, the Spaniards calling none so but them.[1] But in 1654 the Irish Officers having private notice that their own King wished them to quit the Spanish service for the French, they left the Spaniards and came to the French. In 1655, Cromwell having entered into alliance with France, King Charles the Second quitted that country, and in 1656 came into Flanders, then Spanish territory, and employed Ormonde into France to give the Irish regiments notice that they should quit the French and return to the Spanish service. This they were entitled to do under an express article made with the French King's envoy, Du Moulin, at Kilkenny, in 1646, that whenever their own King required their services they should have leave to quit the service of France, and be conducted with their regiments to any place they should choose on the frontiers of France. The loss of ten thousand Irish soldiers, the best men in their army, was of course highly displeasing to Cardinal Mazarin, the minister and governor of France. Accordingly, in hopes of rendering their retirement difficult, he sent as many as

---

[1] "Declaration of the Irish Officers on quitting the Spanish Service for the French in 1654." The several proceedings in Parliament, etc. Printed by Robert Ibbetson, Smithfield, London. 1654. Small quarto.

he could to the theatre of war in Italy. But such was their loyalty to their King, that in a short time five or six regiments were formed out of those lately in the French service, where they left very good conditions, as is recorded in the King's Declaration for the Settlement of Ireland. The Marquis of Ormonde had one of these regiments, the Dukes of York and Gloucester had others, and there were others called after Colonel Grace, Colonel O'Ferrall, Colonel Darcy, Colonel Dempsey, and other Colonels.

The Duke of York's, Colonel Farrell's, and Colonel Grace's regiments continued still embodied at Mardike, in Holland. Great numbers of this class rode in the King's and Duke of York's Lifeguards. Thus, some of them had a present livelihood. The body of them appointed committees to watch over their interests during the concoction of the King's Declaration, by the Agents of the Adventurers and Soldiers, at the Council Board. There they fared badly, being put last for restoration. They remained in London, attending and petitioning while the Act of Settlement was on the anvil in 1662, at the Court at Whitehall, but they did not find their condition mended in the Act of Settlement. And they watched and prayed again in 1664 and 1665, while the Act of Explanation was in contrivance. But this put an end for ever to the hopes and claims of the Irish.

In 1662, the regiments at Mardike were disbanded. The re-formed, or reduced officers, crowded the neighbourhood of Whitehall, seeking for some relief for their distress. In February, 1663, they reminded His Majesty how they had repaired to him in Flanders from their services elsewhere abroad, in 1656, leaving

advantageous employments. They would return, they
said, to try for the aid of their friends in their own
country, if they dared.

But, notwithstanding their fidelity, they feared that
" if they returned to Ireland their arms would be taken
from them, and they thrown into jail on pretence of
their dangerousness." [1]

To this petition they got only a verbal answer
assuring them of His Majesty's care. They waited
until they had pawned and sold all they had, even their
very clothes and arms, to maintain themselves, and
then applied again.[2]

They reminded His Majesty how they were broken
in France, because they acted according to his Orders,
and were made incapable of serving any foreign Prince,
because of their constant adhering to and following
His Majesty's fortunes ; yet, in their own country,
were not trusted with, nor admitted into any employment, military or civil, whereby they might be able to
subsist ; that their estates were enjoyed by those who
got them from the usurpers ; that they were run in
debt for bread and clothes ; some were dead for want,
others in prison for debt, the rest in a starving condition ; all expecting the same misfortune, "unless your
Majesty will, at last, effectually restore your Petitioners
to their said estates, which the Earl of Orrery, at the
Council Board, in 1660 (Sir Audley Mervyn then
being joint agent with him, and concurring with him),
did, in your Majesty's presence, promise should be
done in three months, whereas three years are expired." [3]

[1] Calendar of State Papers, " Domestic." 8vo, London, 1860.
[2] Ibid., p. 207.
[3] Manuscript Collections relating to the Act of Settlement, vol. B., p. 418,
in the Record Tower, Dublin Castle.

The delay demanded by the Agents of the Convention, as they reminded the King, was "to enable the possessors of their Estates to have a convenient time to remove themselves, their families, and stocks. Meantime, whilst these possessors have increased their stocks, the Petitioners live in languishing and sad conditions, especially since they lost their employments in your Majesty's service, which was their only stock and livelihood."[1]

They lingered in London on the business of their claims, until the passing of the Act of Explanation, in the year 1665, which made all petitioning vain. It is truly pitiable to trace their descent downwards to very beggary, and many of them (and those not the least fortunate) to death. To close their complainings which, perhaps, have become as wearisome here as they became to the King and his courtiers, and councillors at Whitehall, their last petition follows in full :—

" To THE KING'S MOST EXCELLENT MAJESTY.

" The humble petition of the Officers who served under your Majesty's Royal Ensigns beyond the Sea,

" SHEWETH,

" That most of the Officers who served under your Royall Ensignes beyond sea have perished by famine, since your Majesty's happy restoration, in soliciting for theire Estates, and the few of them that remain are now like to perish by the Plague, haveing not any means to bring them out of this Towne, nor knowcing whither they shall goe.

" Your Petitioners' humble request is that in regard they are but a few in number, and theire estates but

---

[1] Ibid., Vol. D., p. 121.

small, your Majesty will be graciously pleased to put
an end to their sufferings, by ordering that a proviso
may be inserted in this bill to restore the Petitioners to
their former Estates."[1]

The doors of Whitehall need now no longer be
waited at. The Court of Claims, too, was virtually shut
against them. Every gate of hope was closed. But
return to Ireland they must, to rejoin their companions
in misery, and add a fresh batch to the crowds of
unfortunate anxious wretches that sued before the
Commissioners of Claims, or hopelessly wandered near
mansions and domains that had been their father's or
their own.

> Ah, happy hills—ah, peaceful shades—
> Ah, fields beloved in vain !
> Where once their careless childhood strayed
> A stranger yet to pain !

Yet such was the antique loyalty of these poor Irish
Officers, that in 1678, at the time of the disgraceful
plotted Popish plot in England, they again quitted their
service under Louis XIV., at the King's command,
upon the demand of the English House of Commons,
and once more embraced poverty for his sake.[2]  Yet

---

[1] Manuscript Collections, relating to the Act of Settlement, Vol. B.
p. 418, preserved in the Public Record Office, Four Courts, Dublin.

" Major John Neale,　　　　" Lieutenant John Fox,
" Captain Daniel O'Keeffe,　　" Lieutenant Wm. Barry,
" Captain Wm. Tuite,　　　　" Lieutenant Thos. Cusack,
" Captain Terence Byrne,　　" Lieutenant Henry Tuite.
" Captain David Dannan,
" Captain Michael Brett,　　　　　*Reformed Officers.*
" Captain Wm. Stapleton,　　" Captain Charles M'Carthy,
" Captain Walter Butler,　　" Collonell P. Walsh,
" Captain Philip Barry,　　" Collonell Richd. Fitzgerald,
" Lieutenant Richard Barry,　" Collonell Connor O'Driscol."

[2] " A list of the Officers that quitted the French service by his Majesty's
commands, and are here now in town unprovided for.  The names of

the memory of these too faithful, too loyal men, representatives of so great a part of the nation, is to be the sport of the vile slanderers that would describe the Irish of that age as a nation of murderers, parties to an imaginary massacre.

The following are instances of the claims and conditions of Ensignmen. If exemption from participation in the rebellion of Ireland, a loyal service to King Charles the First in England, and to his son and successor Charles the Second in France, Flanders, and elsewhere, could entitle Irishmen to consideration it was the case of Dermot and Owen McCarthy. They were sons of Teige ; and on their father's death, in 1636, were sent beyond sea for their education. Upon the breaking out of the Civil War in England, Dermot, the elder of these brothers, joined the King's army and rose to be Major under Sir Thomas Glenham, Governor of Oxford, in 1644. Sir Thomas had succeeded Sir Arthur Aston in this post, when Sir Arthur, by a fall from his horse, near Bullingden Heath, adjacent to Oxford, broke his leg, which had to be cut off, and was replaced by a wooden one. In 1648, when the King's cause was totally lost in England, Sir Arthur led the flower of the English veterans to Ireland, and by Ormonde's order, garrisoned Drogheda. In this army was Dermot McCarthy, who fell at the head of his troop of horse at the siege of that town by Cromwell. The title to the estates of Dermot devolved on Owen, as his brother and heir. Owen served King Charles

Captains, Lieutenants, and Ensigns follow, including Officers in Ireland unprovided for. There are not only Fitzgeralds, Talbots, Sarsfields, and others of English blood, but McCarthys, Sheehys, Scullys, O'Briens, O'Connors, Dwyers, and others of pure Irish descent. C. P., cc.

the Second abroad in several nations and armies until 1656, when the King called all his subjects to his Ensigns (or banners), out of France into Flanders. Owen then quitted "a very beneficial quality" in France, and came into Flanders, and the King gave him a company in the Duke of York's regiment. In this service he was twice taken prisoner and stript of all, and served faithfully till the late reducement, and then sought (but in vain), to be restored to his father's lands in the baronies of Muskerry and Kerricurrihy, in the county of Cork.[1]

William (Fleming) Lord Slane, served under Ormonde in Ireland as Captain of Horse. He accepted the Peace, and constantly adhered to it. When Cromwell's power prevailed, he came abroad and became Colonel of an Irish regiment, and served the French King in Italy. From thence he made offers to Ormonde and others, his own King's Ministers at Brussels, to bring over his regiment to the Spanish service and join it to the rest of the King of England's forces in the Low Countries. But the King being put to great straits to maintain the forces he then had, he delayed to give Lord Slane an order which alone prevented him from coming. Randal (Fleming), his son and successor, not having taken any lands in Connaught, was ordered all such of his lands as were not in the hands of Adventurers and Soldiers.

Major John Neale served in England where, in the west country, he lost the use of his left hand serving in

---

[1] Privy Seal, July 8th, 1662, C.P., xlii. 351. The names are Cloghroe, Clogh-philip, in Muscry and Balligarvan, in Kerrycurrihy, Ballyna. containing 36 Ploughlands. The contents 2,507 acres, Statute measure. See Townland Index of 1871.

the quality of a Cornet of Horse to Lord Goring, and was otherwise several times wounded in that service, wherein he continued for three years till the army was forced to lay down arms in Cornwall.[1] From thence he went to the King at Jersey, afterwards to France, and continually served in the Duke of York's regiment as a Captain, and after as Major. He went with His Royal Highness from France into Flanders, where he always served His Royal Highness both at Sea and Land. He sought a proviso for his restitution to his estate descended from his ancestors,—which he did not get.[2]

Daniel O'Sullivan More, Esq., declared he had served the King loyally in the late war. Having (he said) a great charge of motherless children and no means, he was reduced (he continued) to a deplorable condition. He had the Earl of Inchiquin's and the late Earl of Clancarty's testimonials, and prayed Ormonde for a farm under his Grace in Kerry.[3]

Donogh McFineen, of Glaneroughty, in Kerry, was another chief of the O'Sullivans. He was (he said), "neither Letteree, Nomince, nor Pinchioner" (pensioner). By Ormonde's orders as Lord Lieutenant

[1] Privy Seal, Feb. 26, 1661. P. R. O. Ireland.

> From Gloucester siege till arms laid down
> In Truro's fields, I, for the Crown
> Under St. George marched up and down,
> And then, Sir,
> For Ireland came, and had my share
> Of blows not lands gained in that war,
> But God defend me from such fare
> Again Sir.

The Moderate Cavalier, Printed at Cork, 1674.

[2] Liber B. Collections concerning the Act of Settlement. Public Record Office, Four Courts, Dublin.

[3] C. P. lx., 259.

in 1649, he had raised a regiment of foot and a troop of horse, and served faithfully under the Earl of Clancarty, until Clancarty laid down arms at Ross Castle (on the Lake of Killarney), in 1652. At the Restoration, on Ormonde's return to Kilkenny, with his Duchess in 1662, he waited on him (he said), at the Castle, there to congratulate him, but he held it unbecoming on that occasion to importune him. Fortune had frowned on him (added McFineen). His health hindered him from waiting on Ormonde at Whitehall, and then (24th November, 1674), having neither farm nor stock, and nothing to maintain his charge, he prayed his Grace's relief before he was quite fallen, and in delicate terms suggested he might be granted some of his former estate in his Grace's hands, or elsewhere in Kerry.[1]

The case of the three brothers Charles, Roger, and Francis Farrell, exhibits the loyalty and sufferings of the Ensignmen in a striking light.

In 1665, Captain Charles Farrell petitioned the Lord Lieutenant and Council in behalf of himself and his brothers Roger Farrell and Francis Farrell, all sons of James Farrell, of Ballyvaghan, in the County of Longford, Charles being his eldest son and heir. Charles had never been in Ireland from the 28th of April, 1641, until his Majesty's happy restoration, and never involved in the rebellion, but, on the contrary, served His Majesty and his royal father in the wars of England, in which service he was taken prisoner, and afterwards banished by the usurpers into foreign parts,

---

[1] Letter dated "Glanereghty," the 24th of November, 1674, Signed "Donagh McFinyn," Endorsed in Ormonde's hand. "Mr. McFinyn." C. P. xxxviii., 113.

where he and his brothers betook themselves to His Majesty's service. From time to time, and more particularly when the petitioner, Charles, served in St. Gillain, His Majesty was pleased to send his orders for their service, whereupon he immediately obeyed and served His Majesty.

Upon the Restoration, the King gave him his Letters to be restored to his estate. This was denied him, but the Lord Lieutenant and Council ordered him one year's rent, of which, however, he only received £20, being ordered off with his company to Tangier, and so could not attend to the prosecution thereof. He and his brothers continued at Tangier till the latter end of August, 1663 ; and there, notwithstanding the petitioners were reduced, and only paid off until the 4th of May previous, they did war, and were engaged in the fight against the Moors on the 24th of June following, in which service the petitioners, Charles and Roger, were sore wounded.[1] When they returned from Africa, the time for claiming "Innocence" before the Commissioners of the Court of Claims was expired, but Charles, with great difficulty, by reason of the opposition of the Protestant Cavaliers who served the King in Ireland before 5th of June, 1649 (commonly called the forty-nine Officers), and who claimed to have the County of Longford as part of their security to satisfy their arrears, got a proviso in the Act of Explanation to be restored.[2]

Eleven years afterwards, however, he was still wandering about seeking help to recover his estate, as

[1] Collections concerning the Act of Settlement, Vol. F., p. 265, P. R. O., Dublin.

[2] 17 and 18 Chas. II. (Irish), chap. 2, sec. 118.

appears by the King's Letter of 12th January, 1667, who therein laments that so well-deserving an officer had as yet had no benefit of the King's Letters, nor of the Act of Parliament, and begging Ormonde and the Council to exert any powers they might be invested with on his favour.[1]

Another of these Ensignmen was Lord Castleconnell. William Bourke, Lord Baron of Castleconnell, in the county of Limerick, hard by the falls of the Shannon, was a kinsman of the Duke of Ormonde's. In the last general " rising out" of the kingdom at the Marquis of Ormonde's commands in 1650, to oppose the advance of Cromwell's forces, Lord Castleconnell, for his birth and possessions, was elected by the gentry of the county of Tipperary to command their levy.[2] When the common calamitie (as he says himself in his petition to his Majesty, July 1, 1662,) disabled him to give other demonstration of his loyalty to his Majesty than the service of his bare and humble person, he betook himself to the King's standards beyond sea. At the Restoration he returned, and waited in hopes to be restored, but his Majesty being full of business (as Lord Castleconnell modestly suggests), did not admit the consideration of his suppliant's concerns. He was named, however, in the King's gracious Declaration, among those to be restored as having faithfully served under the King's Ensigns beyond the seas.[3] While in the greatest indigence (he continued), he served " your Royal Majestie five or six

---

[1] Carte Papers, Bodleian Library, vol. xliii., p. 334.

[2] Letter of the gentry of the county of Tipperary to the Marquis of Ormonde, Lord Lieutenant of Ireland, dated " Ahacotty, March 25, 1650." C. P. xxvii. 133.

[3] 14 & 15 Charles II. (Irish), chap. 2, King's Declaration, sec. 26.

years in the Netherlands, trailing a pike in the Duke of York's regiment (*i.e.*, as a common soldier), he understood no miserie. But now he has run in debt for food and raiment, and is at the end of his credit, in imminent hazard of imprisonment for his debts, and unable further to subsist if your Majestie relieve him not."[1]

In pity of his fallen fortunes, and in the difficulty of restoring him to his estates, the Duke of Ormonde prevailed with the King to grant him a temporary pension of £1,000 a year. On the 3rd April, 1667, in thanking Lord Ormonde for this seasonable relief, he opens his sad case to him, baffled, as he finds himself, even of this alleviation, by the delays and tricks of Sir Daniel Bellingham of the Treasury.

"My Lord (he proceeds), as my father, who pretended the honour of a near relation to your Grace and the Duchess's family, and by the means of your ancestor, Thomas Earl of Ormonde, was bred in his house, who recovered his estate and the honour for him, I doe take the presumption to open my miserable condition to your Grace, and doe expect no less favour from you, having ever found your Grace's willingness to look on persons of my condition in these sad times.

"I am confident your Grace knows how faithfully I have served H. M. and your Grace at home and abroad, and am during my life resolved to dispose of myself as your Grace shall think fitt. Therefore I humbly beg your Grace's pardon that I plainly open my unfortunate grievance ; for, on my word, my Lord, I was forced, as Captain Henesy can inform your

---

[1] Carte Papers, vol. xlii., p. 376.

Grace, to pawn the very clothes I had for £20, to bring me out of Dublin, and ever since I am in so great a povertie, that if I had a mind to wait on your Grace, I am not able to appeare for want of cloathes—my wife and children being ready to forsake house and home, and all the little stocke I had, being taken for rent. Sir Valentine Browne and Sir Edward Fitzharris, being engaged for what monies brought me for Ireland, are like to suffer for me. Therefore, being not able to waite on your Grace to present my humble petition, I took the bouldness to write these uncouth lines, begging of your Grace to send Sir George Lane or Secretary Page to Sir Daniel Bellingham, to cause him to see me satisfied my arrears, if your Grace shall so think fit, and your Grace will ever oblige him that is

" Your Grace's

" Most obedient faithful servant,

" CASTLECONNELL."

" Castledrobid,[1]

" April 3, 1667."

So great, however, were the numbers of the distressed nobility and gentry seeking some respite from starvation by the Pension List, that before 1675 Lord Castleconnell's pension was reduced to £100 a year, and this so badly paid, that at Michaelmas, 1680, it was two years in arrear, together with pensions of like amount to Lord Netterville, Lord Trimleston, Lord Upper Ossory, Lord Dunboyne, Lord Brittas, Lord

---

[1] Carte Papers, vol. xxxv. p. 225. Castledrobid was Castletown, near Celbridge, in the County Kildare, built in the 18th Century by the Right Hon. Thomas Connolly. But in the 17th, in 1667, it was the estate of Sir William Dungan (made Viscount Dungan in 1661, and subsequently Earl of Limerick), where, no doubt, Lord Castlconnell was Lord Dungan's guest.

Louth, Sir William Talbot, Lord Roche's children, and others.[1]

But Lord Castleconnell was not the only man of rank and late of estate obliged to hide for want of clothes to appear abroad in. Hundreds were in the same plight,—fathers, mothers, daughters, sons. Colonel Charles MacCarthy Reagh of Kilbrittan Castle, near Bandon, in the County of Cork, was once the owner of a principality. The ruins of Kilbrittan and of other dependent Castles near the Bandon river attest the former splendour of the MacCarthy Reaghs. Colonel Charles MacCarthy had married the sister of the Earl of Clancarty, Ormonde's brother-in-law. He was named among the Ensignmen as having served the King in foreign parts ; but finding no provision made for the Ensignmen in the Act of Explanation, he besought Ormonde to save from utter ruin an ancient loyal family related to his Grace. He (Colonel Charles MacCarthy Reagh), his wife, the Earl of Clancarty's sister, and their seven children were (he said) in a most sad and deplorable condition, himself and his wife and some of his children being forced for want of means or habitation to repair to Dublin, where they were then destitute even of necessary clothes to appear in, not having penny or penny's worth to relieve them, but in the words of truth (added Colonel MacCarthy), in a condition ready to perish with starving ; and such of them as were in the country, he said, had no other being or subsistence than wandering from house to house looking for bread. He prayed the Duke to stretch forth his hand of mercy and prevent the miser-

[1] C. P. iii., 225.

able ruin that threatened a house and family ever so
endeared to his Grace's ancestors, and to preserve the
lives of his wife and children and the estate of a loyal
family who (under God) had no other hope than his
Grace.[1]

Another, late of great Estate, was in like condition
with Colonel MacCarthy Reagh. This was Lord
Clanmalier.

Lewis Dempsey (or O'Dempsy), Viscount Clanmalier, commanded as Colonel a regiment of foot
under Ormonde in 1649 and 1650. From time before
the English invasion the O'Dempsys were seated at
the head waters of the Barrow, which there divides
the King's county from the Queen's county. On the
North side, in the King's county, their chief house
was Ballybrittas ; in the Queen's county they owned
the territory round what is now called Portarlington.
The O'Dempsys had not only intermarried with the
Nugents and Fitzgeralds, but Lewis's eldest brother,
to whom he succeeded as heir, had married Cleopatra
Cary, a near kinswoman of Sir Henry Cary, Viscount
Falkland, Lord Lieutenant of Ireland from 1622 to
1629. In October, 1652, Lewis, Lord Clanmalier,
was tried at the High Court of Justice at Kilkenny
for murder committed by his soldiers in surprising
Maryborough in 1641, and burning the town. He
amused the Court by his simplicity. He had never
been in such a place before, he said, and wondered
why that little man (Wm. Basil, the Attorney-General) was so vindictive against him. He confessed that
he came with 400 men to surprise the fort, and was

---

[1] Petition of Charles MacCarthy Reagh, Esq. (A.D. 1665.)  C. P. xxxv.,
137.

angry with them for burning the town instead. As the killing of soldiers in arms would be no murder, but the death of simple townsmen would, and as this was against his intention they spared him, but kept him close prisoner at Dublin till the King's restoration. On 15th March, 1665, as he wrote to Ormonde, he was in so sad and poor a condition that he had not means to wait upon him, or employ another to solicit for him. It is to be observed he was no Ensignman ; for, being in prison, he could not resort to the King's standard abroad. He could not claim Innocence, for he had dwelt in the Irish quarters. But he was entitled as an Article man to claim the benefit of the Peace of 1648. He had been excommunicated (he said) by the Nuncio, tried by Cromwell's High Court of Justice for his life, and with much hazard escaped that danger, and was afterwards kept prisoner for six years. He had nothing left, he added, to live upon, but hoped through Ormonde for a proviso in the new bill to restore him to his Estate.

It will be seen hereafter how it was granted to Sir Henry Bennett, afterwards made Earl of Arlington.

By the King's Declaration of 30th November, 1660, embodied in the Act of Settlement, there were Thirty-six Nominees besides the Sixteen Sufferers from the violence of the Nuncio, specially named for restoration to their estates, after reprisal given to the Adventurers and Soldiers in possession.

But as there was no fund for reprising, this provision was a fraud. By the Act of Explanation, however (passed 24th December, 1665), the Adventurers and Soldiers were to surrender one-third. The Nominees, now fully expecting to remedy their position by this

enlargement of the fund for reprisals, got a Clause
that they should be restored, not to their whole Estate,
but only to their Chief Houses with 2,000 acres of land
contiguous. Each now in joy selected his contiguity,
and there may still be seen lists of the Contiguities of
the Nominees. But by a new provision in the same
Act, Protestants were to be first provided for, and
those parts of the Act first put in execution that
might most benefit them, as their interest was the
King's greatest care.[1] Between these two provisions
not one of the Nominees was ever restored, though
some got back by decrees of Innocence or by special
provisoes in the Act of Explanation. By another provision, any Adventurer or Soldier who had given up
his land to the Irish proprietor too readily, on view of
the King's Privy Seal, just after the overthrow of the
Usurpers rule, was to be restored by the Commissioners of the new Court.[2] The case of Walter Tuite
exhibits the effect of this enactment. The Tuites
were an ancient Anglo-Norman family, barons of Hugh
De Lacy's palatinate of Meath, not then divided into
East and West Meath. Cullanmore, Tuite's castle,
was adjacent to Mullingar. Andrew Boy Tuite,
Walter's father, as an opponent of the Nuncio, was, in
1647, made a prisoner of by Owen O'Neill, that champion of the Church, and he was only yielded up on the
pressing entreaties of the Supreme Council of the
Confederate Catholics. He got back Cullanmore,
through a King's Letter at the Restoration, when the
Cromwellians did not as yet know their strength, and
did not dare to refuse. Upon Andrew Boy Tuite's

[1] Clauses v. and vi.
[2] Clause xi.

death Cullanmore devolved upon Walter as his heir and remainder man. Walter got himself inserted among the Nominees in the New Act. But the Adventurer turned him and his family out under the provision just named, after they had been for four years seated again by their ancient fireside, rejoicing, probably, in their happier lot, now rendered all the bitterer.

In his petition to the Duke of Ormonde in the year 1666, he states, that neither he nor his deceased father accepted any lands from the usurpers in Connaught. His father was restored to part of his estate under His Majesty's Letters in the year 1661, which he (the petitioner) continued to hold until that he was dispossessed by an Injunction from the Commissioners of Claims two days before May last. His family, he says, " have no residence at present by reason of his giving up possession, which is already the loss of his Stock, the loss of his Cropp of Corne (which the Adventurer immediately seized upon) and the ruine of himself and family.

" That he had been constantly resident in this Citty of Dublin this twelve months of Saturday last, having not sixpence this halfe year past to relieve him.

" That one of his sons, within a month after they lost their possessions, through cold and want, sickened, and was then on the point of death, given over by the doctors, without any hope of recovery.

" That his eldest son for want of any other place of residence, or anything to relieve him, followed him to that City, where he sickened also, and was a month past in the hands of doctors, but now began to mend if he had wherewith to relieve him.

" That his mother, daughter, and two other of his
sons were ever since May last ranging, the Lord knew
where ; having not a bit to put in their mouths.

" He therefore prayed the Duke to take pity of his
most miserable condition in giving him some present
relief, as also to recommend him to the Commissioners
of the Court of Claims, that he might be one of the
first Nominees that they should settle in his 2,000
acres. And the rather that there was not any of the
Nominees in so bad a condition, having for the most
part of them got lands in Connaught, and the rest of
them some other grants or lands by way of Custodiam,
or otherwise to relieve them."[1] But the Duke could
do nothing for him. For, before he could be restored,
the Cromwellian in possession must be reprised, and
there was no land to reprise him with.

[1] C. P. ix., 267.

# PART SECOND.

## CHAPTER I.

To sketch the history and generation of the tories of Ireland, one ought to go up to the re-plantation of Ireland in the reign of the Catholic Sovereigns, Philip and Mary, in the King's and Queen's Counties.

It was in mercy to the O'Moores and O'Connors and five other septs or stocks—the Kellys, the Lalors, the Dorans, the M'Evoys, the Doolans,—that Sir Arthur Chichester, in 1608, transplanted the remains of them to Munster after eighteen rebellions in forty years, lest "the White Moores" (as he called them) should be utterly extirpated. By this nickname of the White Moors, Sir Arthur alluded to the gross breach of faith of the King of Spain in driving out the Moors of Andalusia in 1609, contrary to the treaty made with the remnants of that race after their rebellion in a former reign, the consequence being that for 230 years after, these Moors became the pirates of Algiers, and Sallee Rovers in hatred of the injustice of the Christians. Another motive was to prove to the Irish and to the world the capacity of England to undertake the Ulster plantation, then in hand. " If we cannot compass the transplantation of the O'Moores and O'Connors, how can we plant Ulster ? If we can, the world will see that we shall accomplish the new planting of Ulster." The very same feelings drove the Irish tories to the mountains and the forests.

The next accession to the ranks of the Irish tories was the agrarian revolution attempted by King James the First in Ulster.

Ten years after the plantation of Ulster (A.D. 1619), Lord Deputy St. John "finds the younger sons of gentlemen who have no means of living, and will not work, going to the woods to maintain themselves by the spoil of the quiet subjects, for he had not heard of any men of quality (he said), or that had anything of his own among them." Within three years 300 of them had been killed by natives, or hanged by martial law. But they grew so fast that in 1622, Captain Neale, Captain Donnelly, Captain Delahoide, and Captain Maguire, were allowed to raise as many as would follow them to the service of the King of Spain.

The plantation of Wexford produced other tory outbreaks, and Captain James Butler, from the King of Poland, in 1619, got warrant to bring away with him for the King of Poland's service, Donogh M'Kane (Kavanagh), John O'Phelan, and Edward M'Morrys (Kavanagh), and others, from the woods of Lower Leinster; and St. John would willingly give any foreign prince ten thousand of them for a war abroad. For Morris M'Edmond Kavanagh, a bastard of that ever rebellious race of the Kavanaghs, with a crew of wicked rogues, as wicked as himself, surprised Sir James Carroll's and Mr. Marwood's houses, in the Wexford plantations, murdered their servants, burnt their towns—for which outrage, however, most of them were since slain or executed by martial law. The plantation of Fercal, in the King's County, and the plantation of Leitrim, produced others. As evil begets evil, all these plantations led to the great and overwhelming Cromwellian plantation or Settlement (as it was called, though it might be more properly called an Un-settlement), and the counter Revolution at the King's Restoration produced more.

Some few particulars or instances of hardship and injustice have been already given that may prepare for the abundant crop of outrages to follow from the same causes. Roger Boyle, Lord Broghill of Cromwell's day, was one of the arch-regicide's trustiest supporters. He had strongly urged Cromwell " to king himself," yet did not hesitate to become the king's right-hand man at the Restoration. His price was that he should be secured in the confiscated lands of the Irish he had acquired from Cromwell.

Broghill was Irish born, was of a literary as well as a martial turn, and understood Ireland and Irishmen thoroughly. He had no delusions about the Act of Settlement. Nor did he expect it to produce peace or settlement, knowing his countrymen so well as he did. " When I consider (said he in his " Irish Colours Displayed," being an answer to Father Peter Walsh's " Irish Colours Folded,") when I consider the former forfeitures, and what quantities are now to be disposed of, besides how perpetual a memory the Irish retain of those (by them) esteemed injuries . . . and their resolutions even in cold blood to unravel the settlements of ages past," he feared the contest between the two parties in Ireland would never have end, however it might shock the Duke of Ormonde, to whom he dedicated the work, and others, as an uncharitable thought.

Among other circumstances leading him to that sad

conclusion he said was the custom of the Irish in their funerals after their savage manner, to rehearse among the praises of the defunct the number of English murdered by him or his ancestors, either as soldiers in war or as Woodkerns or tories in peace, as described so well by Edmund Spenser, and used to Orrery's day in the wild parts of the north, where they had no witnesses but themselves.

Another consideration inducing the same belief was the persistent conduct of the many Roman Catholic gentlemen restored to their homes and lands by the King, because of their service in his forces abroad. " Not a man of them (says Orrery) was content to save his own stake, to break from the herd, or leave stickling in the patronage and defence of the common party." He had often deplored, he added, that his birth or his fortunes should have been cast into an age or country " where men could not live together more like the sons of one father, the subjects of one Prince, the servants of one God, than he saw they were likely to do."

Some of the Catholic gentry of old English blood, Talbots, Cusacks, Plunkets, Cheeverses, got back some of their ancient lands through the King's favour.   But the greater part even of these were reduced to poverty, and the native Irish proprietors of Ulster were so universally.  And for thirty years after the Restoration, Ulster was the most disturbed part of the kingdom, that part where (to use the Duke of Ormonde's expression), there were the worst Protestants and the worst Papists in Ireland, the Presbyterians being anti-Prelatists, and the Papists (through being stript of their lands universally), the most disturbed and rebellious.

But all four Provinces were more or less disturbed by tories.

In 1670, Primate Plunket summoned a General Synod of the Irish Church, which met at Mr. Reynolds's House in Bridge Street, Dublin, at the foot of the Bridge, on 16th June. One of its Statutes ordered all priests and preachers to warn their people against giving aid to tories. In the month of October following, Primate Plunket sought out in the woods and mountains many of the best families, who being reduced to poverty and desperation by losing their properties, had turned tories. These he brought back to better courses, and having obtained their pardon, accompanied them himself to Dublin, and saw them ship themselves on board vessels bound for France. In an account of the state of the county of Kildare in 1684, the plains were described as tilled by peasants; but the woods, bogs, and fastnesses were said to be the harbours and shelter of robbers, tories, and wood-kerne, usually the offspring of gentlemen who having mis-spent or forfeited their estates, and therefore without means, yet deemed trade too mean and base for a gentleman. They were *nussled up* (nursed) by their priests and followers in the opinion that they would yet recover their lands to live in their predecessors splendour.

In this opinion they remained till the accession of King James the Second, and then they made an attempt at a Counter-Revolution, which signally failed. They displayed the usual political incapacity of the Irish. Though warned by their best friends of the danger of alienating not only the Cromwellian Protestants, but the many Catholic purchasers, they would repeal the Act of Settlement before Derry and Enniskillen were taken. And the consequence was, the Penal Laws, with the aim of reducing the Irish Catholics to the state of Gibeonites, hewers of wood, and drawers of water to the English of Ireland. Influence (said Chief Justice John Gore, Earl of Annaly, Chief Justice of the King's Bench, in the case of M'Carthy against Hanly in 1771), influence was found to follow property, and the design of the penal laws was to prevent the Irish from acquiring any property beyond what they were possessed of at the passing of those laws in the first year of the reign of Queen Anne. The Act of Parliament, he adds, was made by those who had suffered so severely during the short reign of King James the Second, and by the disturbances which afterwards followed, and did not want resentment for the injuries they suffered, and a resolution to prevent their posterity from suffering the like injuries by lessening the Irish interest in the Kingdom.

By another Statute their landed property was made to moulder away in their hands by the gavelling clause, dividing the lands of an Irish father equally among his sons, notwithstanding any will he might make. And by subsequent Statutes eldest sons were induced to become Protestants, as they thereby secured the family estate to their own use at their father's death, a provision so much admired by the first English historian of the present day.

But all these provisions were as nothing in their effects until the Statute was passed giving the family estate in the hands of an Irishman to the first Protestant Discoverer. It was this that animated the Popery Acts. Sons now filed bills against their fathers, tenants against their landlords, and common Protestant Discoverers levied black mail wherever they found estates held secretly in trust by an Englishman, in other words, a Protestant, for an Irishman. Till, at length, the Irish owners of landed estate deemed it best to conform to English Religion,—though still in danger of being betrayed by servants or others if they practised their religion in secret, thereby becoming "Lapsed Papists." In one case a domestic servant swore he observed his master reading every morning after breakfast, and, on looking under the chair cushion, in his master's absence, he found it to be a manual of Catholic devotion. Others swore they saw Serjeant Meade, then holding an Assize Court at Cork, at Chapel, at Mass.

They had rather trust themselves for one moment to the mercy of God, by a little perjury, they said, than their estates to any Protestant as their trustee at the risk of Protestant Discoverers.

Meantime the dispossessed proprietors wandered about their former abodes, seeking charity from the new inhabitants of their estates, or boldly turned tories. The Irish peasantry never refused them hospitality, but allowed them to " cosher on them," as it was called, giving them a certain number of days' board and lodging.

Archbishop King complains of the number of them thus supported, or by stealing and torying.

These pretended Irish gentlemen, together with the numerous coshering Irish Clergy that lived much after the same manner, were the two greatest grievances of the kingdom in this Archbishop's view, and more especially hindered its settlement and happiness. The

Archbishop and the new possessors of the lands of these poor Irish gentlemen complained of their pride and idleness in not becoming their labourers. But the sense of injustice and their use of arms were against it. These were the pretended Irish gentlemen that would not work (as described in the Statute of 1707, "for the more effectual suppression of tories,") but wandered about demanding victuals, and coshering from house to house among their fosterers, followers, and others, and were, on the presentment of any Grand Jury of the County, to be seized and sent on board the Queen's fleet, or to some of the plantations in America.

The story of Daniel O'Keeffe and Mary O'Kelly belongs to this era of treachery, when tory betrayed or murdered tory by inducement of the law. On a hill beside the river Blackwater, nine miles west of Mallow, stands the ruins of the Castle of Dromagh, erected by the O'Keeffes. It guards a pass over the river.

It was near Dromagh that the last battle in Munster was fought in the war of 1641. Hugh O'Keeffe was then the owner,—a firm adherent of Ormonde's and an opponent of the Nuncio's.

For some reason he got the name of " Paschalis." He was made a prisoner in some engagement by Moriertagh O'Brien, a supporter of the Nuncio's, and passed his word not to escape privately. One morning, rising up suddenly in bed, he said,—Gentlemen, I give you notice that I'm off,—and jumping out at the window, escaped, pretending that he had not broken his word, because he had given notice of his intention. For five years after Cromwell's departure from Ireland he kept up war as a tory. His son Daniel raised a troop of horse at his own charge, and fought bravely against Cromwell, but retired to Spain, and thence came to the King's standard in France, and got a foot Company in the Duke of York's regiment, and was desperately wounded in his seven years' service.

Ormonde, immediately after the King's Restoration, used his influence with Orrery to get him restored.

Daniel O'Keeffe's father, said Ormonde, if alive, would have deserved to be restored for his adherence to the peace of '48, and Daniel was well entitled by his father's services and sufferings, as well as his own. And he had taken no land (he added) in Connaught.[1] He was accordingly restored as a Letteree.[2]   And, in 1685, to strengthen his title he got a grant under the Commission of Grace.[3]   His own and his father's loyalty had been so useful to them both that he thought he could never go wrong in being loyal to the rightful king, though a Cromwell or a William of Orange might seem to triumph for a time.

Accordingly, in the war of 1690, he adhered to King James the Second, and after the defeat at the Boyne, was outlawed, and his estate sold in 1703 amongst the other Forfeited Lands at Chichester House.[4]   There is a great cave in the cliff over the Blackwater, called the Outlaw's Cave, because there Daniel O'Keeffe, after being stripped of his lands, led

[1] Ormonde to Orrery, March 2nd, 1660. C. P. xlviii., 11.

[2] King's Letter, February 5th, 1660. C. P. xli., 299. Petition of Captain Daniel O'Keeffe, June 29th, 1663, Liber C, 420, Liber E, 259.

[3] June 10th, 1685. C. P. clxvii., 30.

[4] Roll of 2nd Anne (1703). Dromagh (with other lands to the number of 5,000 acres) late the estate of Captain Daniel O'Keeffe, attainted. Sold by the Trustees of Forfeited Estates, at Chichester House, on College Green, to the Hollow Sword Blade Company. Vol. III. Record Commissioners' Reports (Folio), p. 374.

an outlaw's life, with Mary O'Kelly as his solace. It was Mary O'Kelly that he employed to bring him necessaries from Mallow.

One day, fondling this mistress of his heart on her return, he felt a paper in the bosom of her dress, and, taking it in his hand, he found it was a letter from the Commander of the garrison at Mallow.

It disclosed her treachery.

She had been bought over.

O'Keeffe plunged his *skeane*, or long Irish knife, in her heart.

There is a very imperfect traditional account of Daniel O'Keeffe, but the above is all authentic.[1] The tale is told in an ode of seven stanzas. Among them are the following:

> " No more shall mine ear drink
>     Thy melody swelling ;
> Nor thy beaming eye brighten
>     The outlaw's dark dwelling ;
> Or thy soft heaving bosom
>     My destiny hallow,
> When thine arms twine around me,
>     Young Mauriade'ny Kallagh.

> " The moss couch I brought thee
>     To-day from the mountain,
> Has drunk the last drop
>     Of thy young heart's red fountain,
> For this good *skeane* beside me
>     Struck deep and rung hollow
> In thy bosom of treason,
>     Young Mauriade ny Kallagh."[2]

---

[1] Dublin Penny Journal of 29th August, 1835. Volume IV., Number 165.

[2] Mauriade ny Kallagh is the Irish for Mary O'Kelly. " Ny " was always used instead of " O " in the names of women.

In 1695 a law was made that any tory killing two
other tories, proclaimed and on their keeping, was
entitled to pardon for all former crimes except murder.
Such distrust and alarm now ensued among their
bands on finding one of their number so killed, that it
became difficult to kill a second. Therefore, in 1718,
it was declared a sufficient qualification for pardon for
a tory to kill one of his fellow tories. These Acts
were put in force in the reign of King George III.
They only expired in 1776.

On October 13th, 1713, at the assizes and general
gaol delivery for the Royalties and Liberties of the
County of Tipperary, and the County of Cross Tipperary at Clonmel, the Grand Jury presented Charles
Carroll of Cloncleary, Michael Ro Prendergast, Morris
Boy Prendergast, both of Curraghnemony, and three
others, to be tories, robbers, and rapparees in arms and
out upon their keeping, and the Grand Jury desired
that they might be proclaimed,—and an entry was
made on the affidavit by the Clerk of the Crown of
the names of the Grand Jurors, and of the Presentment having been openly read and confirmed by the
Court.

On the 27th March, 1760, the Grand Jury of the
County of Cork made a similar presentment against
three men of the name of Terry for the murder of
Francis Sullivan, schoolmaster.

These presentments remain in hundreds. No
wonder, therefore, that the name of tory and the sport
of tory-hunting became familiar words. I remember
well how my grandfather, on the mother's side, dwelling

in Palace Row (as the north side of Rutland Square was then called), used to sing for us—

> "Ho! brother Teig, what is your story?
> I went to the wood and shot a tory,
> I went to the wood and shot another:
> Was it the same, or was it his brother?"

> "I hunted him, and I hunted him out,
> Three times through the bog, and about and about,
> Till out of the bush I spied his head,
> So I levelled my gun, and shot him dead."

Well, too, can I remember how my father has told me (who died 31st May, 1846), that his father, a Solicitor and Deputy Registrar of the Court of Chancery, from the County of Tipperary, dwelling, and dying in 1803, in Chancery Lane, Dublin, had seen the proprietor, or his son or grandson, once owner of broad lands, going about as a beggar with his old title deeds tied up in a common cotton handkerchief, these, and the respect paid him by the common Irish, being the only signs left to show the world he was a gentleman. About twenty-five years ago, I was myself shown at the Rolls Office of Chancery, by one of the gentlemen there, a Privy Seal of King Charles the Second, brought thither the day before by some peasant of the county of Longford, descendant of some O'Reilly, ordering his ancestor to be restored to all such of his lands as were not in the hands of Adventurers or Soldiers, of as much real value as if it had ordered him lands in the Moon.

His descendants, occupants of a cabin, had preserved it in cotton-wool as a precious inheritance for 200 years, being the choicest preservative they knew of, though singularly unfit for preserving a paper document. Hundreds of Original Privy Seals of the same class have I seen among the Ormonde papers at the Bodleian Library, Oxford,—the same Venetian hand, with the Privy Seal on paper, on a large wafer stamped at the upper corner of the left hand above the King's sign manual.

SIR CHARLES COOTE, first Earl of Mountrath, was succeeded by his eldest son of the same name, of a much better nature than his father, according to Sir Maurice Eustace. Sir Maurice, in December 1661, the first Earl being not long dead, and Sir Charles, the second Earl, being at his departure for London to wait upon the Duke of Ormonde, Chancellor Eustace recommended him to Ormonde as having gone counter to the late times all along, and since Sir Maurice's return to Ireland had manifested much affection to the poor natives, was of a very sweet disposition, and made of much better mould (mold ?) than his nearest relations.[1]

Between him and the Countess, his stepmother, who shortly after her husband's death married Sir Robert Reading, there arose a contest concerning the late Earl's will that exhibits the unsettlement of property of that period. The late Earl was possessed of Gormanston Castle under a grant from Cromwell, and Lord Gormanston recovered it by the strong hand, and placed sentinels on the walls,—was indicted in 1664, for this forcible entry, but was pardoned—and only recovered complete possession of his estate in 1668, on undertaking to pay all profits since he got into

---

[1] Eustace to Ormonde, Dublin, December 29, 1661. C. P. ccxiv., 200.

possession, to the Countess Dowager of Mountrath. The late Earl of Mountrath having been obliged to surrender the Earl of Clanricarde's house of Tyrellan, and such other Clanricarde lands as he held, the Countess Dowager of Mountrath sought to be reprised for the lands so restored out of Colonel John Fitzpatrick's and Thomas Luttrell's late Connaught assignments. They had been transplanted to Connaught, but their late transplanters allotments were then at the King's disposal in regard that Fitzpatrick and Luttrell were restored to their former estates in Leinster.

The Countess had further differences with her stepson, the second Earl, concerning the new acquired estate of her late dear husband, the first Earl, which she claimed for her four fatherless children, as intended for them by their father. The Earl and his stepmother the Countess, had a hearing of their differences before the King in Council, but the cause was referred to the Lord Lieutenant and Council of Ireland, and they decreed that the whole new acquired estate of the late Earl of Mountrath should be cast into hotch-pot and divided by lot between the heir-at-law, the present Earl, and the children of the second marriage,—a provision which was confirmed by the Act of Explanation.[1]

While the late Earl of Mountrath's will was in dispute, his son and heirs as protector of his father's lands, found that some of the late owners of the new acquired estate were seeking to recover them by getting provisoes inserted in the then pending Act of Expla-

---

[1] Sec. cxxvi.

nation, though their guilt was so great (according to his account), they durst never come to a trial in the late Court of Claims. One of these was Captain Edward Herbert, who claimed as heir-at-law the estate formerly belonging to Sir Jasper Herbert.

These lands lying in the Barony of Ballycowen, in the King's County, the late Earl of Mountrath had purchased from Captain Samuel Bonnell, to whom they had been set out for his arrears. If there was nothing to be objected against Captain Herbert touching the late rebellion, the young Earl of Mountrath declared to Ormonde he did not know that Captain Herbert had the least title to them as heir of Sir Jasper. Besides, it could be proved how active his father and he were in the late Rebellion ; his father at the time of the Pope's Nuncio's residence in Ireland, being High Sheriff of the King's County, he adhered to the Nuncio, and Edward, his son, was in arms with the Irish ; and in England, not many years since, joined Oaky's regiment, against the King.

But Lord Mountrath was more troubled about the Costigans. Their lands lay in the Queen's County, and had been purchased by the late Earl from Major Thomas Davis, who had them set out to him for arrears of pay. Lawrence Costigan, brother of John, claimed as an Innocent in the late Court of Claims, but was decreed Nocent, and his claim dismissed on the 18th of February, 1663.

The Costigans now turned tories, as appears by Ormonde's warrant to Henry Gilbert, High Sheriff of the Queen's County, to hunt John Costigan, Gregory Costigan his brother, Hugh Ro. Kelly, and several others, their comrades abroad in the King's and

Queen's Counties on both sides of the mountain of Slieve Bloom, and on and about the bog of Moneely, in the County of Tipperary. The Sheriff had liberty to employ spies, and assure pardon and reward to any of them that should betray the others.[1] These measures were successful; for Lord Mountrath mentions in his letter that the two brothers had been taken, and one condemned and hanged the week before,—the other reprieved for a few days.[2] .

One of the Costigans, it seems, still evaded capture. For Colonel Grace, a great friend of Ormonde's, writing for a protection and pass for James Dwiggin, to quit the kingdom, Ormonde refused. Dwiggin's estate was one of those in Lord Mountrath's possession as part of the late Earl's new estate, having been set out to Colonel Daniel Abbott for his arrears, and purchased by the late Earl.

His son, then Earl, in his letter to Lane, mentioning the two Costigans' sentence, adds, as for Dwiggin, he stands charged with murthering some of my Lord Duke's servants, as they were going from his Grace to Sir George Hamilton at " Rosgray."

Ormonde, in refusing Colonel Grace's request for Dwiggin of quitting the kingdom, adds, " but if he will bring in the head of the tory Costigan, or some others of that crew, we may be induced to grant him His Majesty's pardon ;[3] which proves that the report of Dwiggin's having murdered some of Ormonde's ser-

---

[1] Warrant dated February 16th, 1664. C. P. cxlv., 269.

[2] Mountrath to Sir George Lane, Ormonde's Secretary. Dublin, June 15, 1664. C. P. xxiii., 257.

[3] Ormonde to Grace, 30th July, 1666. C. P. cxliv., 86.

vants was not true, for murders were always excepted from pardon.[1] When mention was lately made of Lewis O'Demp-sey, Lord Viscount Clanmalier, he was detained in some poor lodging, unable to appear in public for want of fit apparel. He derived a great estate in the King's and Queen's counties, on the upper waters of the Barrow. He held his lands in tail male under the limitations of a Royal Grant to his grandfather, Sir Terence O'Dempsey. Not being indicted or outlawed, for the Sheriff did not dare to venture so far in 1641 to execute his office, his estate tail was not forfeited, and the entail passed to his son, Maximilian O'Dempsey,

---

[1] A list of the names of the former proprietors of the Earl of Mount-rath's new estate :

| | |
|---|---|
| John Duiggin. | Bryan Fitzpatrick. |
| Patrick Kennine. | Teig Fitzpatrick. |
| Patrick Connor. | John Deoran. |
| John Kennine. | Wm. Delany. |

The lands belonging to the above-named persons, lying in the barony of Upper Ossory and Queen's County, were purchased from Colonel Daniel Abbot.

Florence Costigan.

(His father and himself were found Nocent in the Court of Claims—his eldest brother was hanged for murder, and two other of the brothers, Toryes, and now newly taken.)

John Fitzpatrick.
Denis Kenine.
John Cashau.

The lands belonging to the above-named persons, lying in the barony and county aforesaid, were purchased from Major Thomas Davis.

Sir Jasper Herbert.
John Briscoe.
John and Murrogh Conroy.
Hugh Molloy.

The lands, formerly belonging to the persons aforesaid, lying in the King's County and barony of Ballycowen, were purchased from Captain Samuel Bonnell.

Schedule annexed to the Earl of Mountrath's letter of June 15, 1664. C. P. xxxiii., 257.

who was alive at the Restoration, and was married. Sir
Henry Bennett, Lord Arlington, Secretary of State, being
determined apparently to increase his fortune by landed
estate in Ireland, got from the King a grant of Lord
Clanmalier's estate, and formed the King's County
lands into the manor of Charlestown, after his patron,
King Charles the Second, and the Queen's County
lands into the manor of Portarlington, after himself.
He was brother-in-law to the Earl of Ossory, having
married Isabella de Beverweert, Countess of Ossory's
sister. He expected Ossory to promote all his greedy
desires. For, after having got Lord Clanmalier's great
estate, he made an effort to add to it another nearly as
extensive, viz., that of Charles Fitzgerald of Ticroghan,
situated at the head waters of the Boyne, near
Clonard. In 1668, G. Fitzgerald, son of Sir Luke,
died, and left only a daughter, and it was contended
that the estate being in tail mail had reverted to the
King, for want of issue male, though his widow was
pregnant. Ossory urged his father to promote his
brother-in-law's desires, but Ormonde refused, much to
Arlington's chagrin.

Whatever defects there might be in Arlington's
title to Lord Clanmalier's estate, he got them all reme-
died by the Act of Explanation.

Meantime he was troubled with the repeated petitions of Lord Clanmalier, and his son's and daughter-
in-law's petitions, and prayed Ormonde to find some
lands to give them for their support, and thus save
him from the trouble he is exposed to by Mrs.
Dempsey's rhetoric, and the necessities of her father,
Lord Clanmalier.

The usual result,—an outbreak of tories followed

the change of possession from the ancient proprietors
to the new.

In August, 1666, the year of the great tory rebellion,
he wrote to Ormonde, that his tenants had been
threatened, and he prayed for Alderman Deey's foot
company to be stationed there for their relief.

Throughout Leinster it was the same.

On 16th January, 1666, Sir Thomas Harman
informed Ormonde that a band, to the number of one
hundred, had appeared at Leighlin Bridge, in the
County of Carlow, under the command of Anthony,
son of Dennis Kirwan, a smith of Leighlin Bridge.[1]
In March of the same year James Fitzharris of Pol-
monty, in the county of Wexford, was appointed to
follow and apprehend tories in Wexford, Kilkenny,
and Tipperary.[2]   In July, 1670, Sir Edward Massy of
Abbeyleix, one of the Privy Council, had licence to
treat with T. Butler, Piers Fitzharris, Dominic Doyne,
and other tories, to depart the kingdom.

Christopher Ramsay, after several nights lying in
the fields in December last, captured three notorious
tories, and lodged them in Carlow Jail.  The same
night, other tories, their confederates, burned him
to the ground.[3]

James Byrne, employed by Lord Kingston, decoyed
three tories to the fair of St. Margaret's, near Santry,
County Dublin.  Mr. Wm. Hetherington, as appointed,
came to his aid with six men, and Byrne secured one
of the tories, but the crowd beat him and left him for
dead.  And then a Justice of the Peace put him in

[1] C. P. cxliv., 59.
[2] Ib., clxv., 359.
[3] Concordatum (or Privy Council) order for £80.  January 20, 1671.

the stocks with his tory prisoner, and bound over
Hetherington for not capturing the others, though he
pursued them for above a mile.[1]

William Carroll, employed by Sir Theophilus Jones
into the King's and Queen's Counties, and County of
Tipperary, for discovering proclaimed tories, met with
Martin Connor, the great tory, and led him and four
other tories to a place where they were slain; but
Carroll himself was severely wounded. And by his
aid Mr. Wm. Hetherington had arrested several others.[2]

The Duke of Ormonde was in hopes (but in that he
was mistaken) that by the diligence of Captain Martin,
employed by Sir Theophilus Jones, who had taken
about a dozen of them, that the knot of tories in Leinster, and upon the borders of Ulster, was pretty well
broken, or at least would be by the time Sir Jerome
Alexander, who had a Special Commission to try, and
a very special inclination to hang them, had done with
them.[3]

Sir Jerome was the Judge who declined to comply
with the pious fraud by which malefactors indicted for
manslaughter, then punishable with death, unless by
benefit of clergy, refused to adopt the statement of the
Clergyman, in Court, that the prisoner could read, because he read three or four words as taught him
for the occasion, and thus obtained his Clergy, and
putting the prisoner on at the next passage, condemned him to death, because he could not, of course,
read the passage.

---

[1] 26th July, 1667. Petition of W. Hetherington. C. P. cliv., 100.
[2] Petition of W. Carroll, with Sir Theophilus Jones's Certificate, dated 28th Feb., 1667.
[3] Ormonde to Orrery, January 16, 1666. C. P. xlviii., 32.

# Chapter III.

## Munster Tories.

" Would to God (said Orrery, in 1664,) we had some
vent for the many loose people who having served
abroad, will not work at home, and therefore live upon
robbery to the great detriment of the public." He
wished one thousand of them might be sent to serve in
Portugal. He forgot to add that these men had
returned home from serving the King in Flanders,
France, and Italy, to find that the lands where they
and their families had dwelt, were in possession of the
Cromwellians. Orrery himself was possessed of
Maurice Lord Roche, of Fermoy's estate, named after
one of the earliest Anglo-Norman settlers De Cogan'
Rathgoggan. And Orrery's new house there being
founded on the first anniversary of the King's
restoration, he called it, he said, Charleville, instead of
its original barbarous name. Orrery was made Lord
President of Munster for life, and his State Letters are
full of the disturbances created by the tories who
subsisted as well as they could in the fastnesses of
Kerry and Cork; In 1666, the tories were running
out in arms in Munster, as well as in Connaught, big
with hopes of that eventful year as they imagined it.

Thus, on the 6th March, 1666, Thomas Sadleir, the
High Sheriff of Tipperary, was authorized to parley
with Laurence Butler, and Nicholas and William Croke,
rebels then in action, and others of a like kind in the
neighbourhood, and to give them protection on their

undertaking to be serviceable, and to bring to justice any other rebels or malefactors.

Similar warrants were given by Ormonde at the same time to Colonel William Warden, authorising him to give licenses to such as he should think fit to go amongst the tories in Tipperary and Waterford, and Queen's County, and to pretend to be of their party, the better to discover their ways. And to promise them pardon (for all except murder), and reward beside. On the 23rd of March following, a Congregation at Mass in Kerry, used such insolent deportment that they rescued a tory. Ormonde accordingly required Lord Orrery to arrest the priest, and such of more than common quality as looked on. This was not so bad, however, as the rage of some tories in the county of Cork, some twenty years later. Some inhabitants of Macroom having apprehended some tories that stood upon their keeping, and prosecuted them to conviction and execution, their confederates and relatives within six days after burned down the town. On the petition of the inhabitants, who had lost goods to the value of £3,000, the several Archbishops of Ireland were requested (June 21, 1683), to promote subscriptions for their relief.

The principal tory of Munster seems to have been Colonel Power. On the march of the troops to the north of Ireland on the occasion of the rebellion in Scotland in 1685, Power, said Lord Longford, grew very active ; for last week he cut out the tongue and cut off the ears of one he suspected of giving information against him. He had committed several considerable robberies, and very narrowly missed of taking Sir John Meade (the Chief Justice of the Royalties and Liberty of Tipperary for Ormonde), but instead took his brother-in-law, and robbed him of eighty pounds. His party was twenty strong, and he intended to increase it, having taken up numbers of the best horses in the county, and he was grown so insolent as to threaten the minister and people of Dungarvan who had spoken against him.[1] But Colonel Power having died shortly after, they found the robbers were worse, and so much increased, that there appeared in one party in the county of Clare, twenty-eight horsemen and twenty foot.[2]

[1] Aungier, Earl of Longford, to Ormonde, Dublin, June 15th, 1685. C.P. ccxvii., 538.

[2] Stewart Lord Mountjoy to Ormonde, Dublin, 16th December, 1685. Ibid. 127.

# CHAPTER IV.

In Connaught, the chief seat of the tories was Mayo and Leitrim. Mayo and Leitrim were two counties reserved from the transplanted Irish by the orders of the Parliament of the Commonwealth,—Mayo as having such fine harbours as Belmullet and Killalla, which offered opportunities to an enemy's shipping,—Leitrim, because of its fastnesses.

In the rest of the province many of the old proprietors remained intermingled with the transplanted from Munster and Leinster after the Restoration. For into this province were thrust by the Cromwellians all the proprietors of the other provinces. At the Restoration, all that had influence enough to get back their ancient lands, quitted that prison, but some remained and founded families that subsist there to this day on the land given them in exchange for their own, as the Talbots of Mount Talbot, the Cheevers and the Fitzgeralds of Turlough, the Bellews of Mount Bellew. But all these were Catholics of old English blood, transplanted many of them only for their religion. They were thus not hostile to the natives like the Puritan Cromwellian Officers and Soldiery in the rest of the kingdom. Nor were there the same number of proprietors stript and rendered desperate through poverty as in the three other provinces. Mayo had been largely granted in Queen Elizabeth's reign to the Binghams, the Ormsbys, the Gores, and others.

F

Leitrim was planted in the reigns of James the First and Charles the First. Jamestown was built as a retreat for the Leitrim planters, and walled to secure them in case of insurrection. Sir Charles Coote the elder, in 1621, undertook the building of the walls, in consideration of receiving the fines or purchase money of the Settlers in Leitrim.

It was to be another Londonderry for the planters. Yet Leitrim in 1667 was so infested by tories that no planters could stay there. "The little rebels known here by the name of tories (wrote Ormonde to Sir Henry Bennett, Lord Arlington),[1] do grow as fast as they are cut off, and have rendered the whole county of Leitrim useless to the King and uninhabitable by any English.

In 1668, Captain Thomas Caulfeild, of Dunammon, by the Shannon, writes to Ormonde that all Connaught was quiet except Leitrim and Mayo, where there were two nests of tories. Those of Leitrim were few, but in Mayo they were about twenty, most of them Ulster men, headed by a bastard of O'Connor Dun. All the art of the army could not compass their taking, they were so harboured by the country. They had lately killed two Scotchmen, and Captain Caulfeild, Vice-President of Connaught, a brother of Lord Charlemont's, suggested the repairing and garrisoning of Balliclare, in the heart of their walks.[2]  In the same year they murdered Captain Gore, and robbed Dr. Dodwell, and fled through the country without any hue and cry raised, or notice given until they were out of

[1] Feb. 27, 1667. O. P. li., 201.
[2] Ib. xxxvi., 5.

reach.[1] The Lord Lieutenant and Council ordered soldiers to be quartered on the septs and kindred of the tories to remain at their charges until the male-factors should be apprehended or cut off by the sword.[2] But the Duke of Ormonde went further, and ordered the arrest of any priest, if a tory was found in his parish, which is more than ever was done in Cromwell's time, said Father Brady, adding, " This Lord Lieutenant will make an end of the Catholics of Ireland if God doth not take him away."[3]

Another method was to give any tories presented by a Grand Jury, or even alleged by the Council Board to have been guilty of any felony, a day to come in and surrender. If after this, they stood upon their keeping, they were declared outlaws, and a price offered for their heads. But if any of them were taken and made amenable, they were to be tried in the ordinary way. Hence, it shocked the Earl of Ossory, then Deputy of his father the Duke of Ormonde, to find that Otway, bishop of Killalla, had done so exorbitant a thing as to execute a tory. It was no way justifiable, said Ossory, for a private man to kill an outlaw, unless he made resistance. There was a design of translating Otway from Killalla to the bishopric of Ossory. And he advised his father against appearing for this unhappy prelate, as it would be a great prejudice to Ormonde's character. " I know not how liable you may be to censure (he concludes), to prefer a clergyman that was

---

[1] Government Correspondence. Domestic Letters. A. 104, p. 13, P. R. O.

[2] Ibid.

[3] Father Patrick Brady to Mr. J. L. Merchant, at Broad Street, London, from Dublin, 29th March, 1679, C. P. lxx., 156.

so indiscreet and violent as to have a tory's head cut off
in his own house when brought in a prisoner."[1]    Yet
Otway became Bishop of Ossory.

Chief of the Connaught or Mayo tories was Colonel
Dudley (or Dualtagh) Costello.    The barony of
Costello was named after the tribe or "nation" of
Dudley Costello.    In the same barony was the great
estate of Viscount Dillon of Costello, called Lough
Glyn.    Both Dillon and Costello pretended to be of
ancient English blood.    Lord Dillon, from being a
Protestant, became a Catholic, and was received into
the Church by the Nuncio himself at Athlone in 1646,
with great ceremony.    He was made by the Confederates President of Connaught.    When the Nuncio
issued his excommunication in 1647, against all that
should serve the Confederates because of the Cessation
or Truce made between them and the Earl of Inchiquin,
Colonel Dudley Costello followed General Owen Ro
O'Neil, then the champion of the Nuncio and the
Church.    In his hatred of the Confederate Government, O'Neil gave his temporary aid to Sir Charles
Coote.    So valuable were Costello's services by taking
many strongholds of men of quality, and making
prisoner of Captain Theobald Dillon, brother of Lord
Dillon of Costello, that Coote suggested to the
Parliament of England that Dudley Costello should be
given a troop in the army.[2]    Colonel Dudley Costello
was among the garrison of the island of Innisbuffin that
surrendered to the Parliament forces in February 1652,

---

[1] Ossory to Ormonde, January 6th, 1680.  Historical MSS. Report.

[2] Sir Charles Coote to the Commissioners for Irish Affairs at Derby
House. Lond 'ndorry, June 11th, 1647. C. P. lxvii., 43.

on the condition that Colonel Cusack, the Governor, Colonel Richard Burke, and Costello, should have liberty to transport 1,000 men for the King of Spain's service. He retired to Flanders, and there rallied to the King of England's standard, became a Captain in the Duke of York's regiment, and gained great distinction for his gallant conduct at the siege of Betune in French Flanders.

At the King's Restoration, he returned to Ireland, and was named among the 250 " Ensignmen " to be restored to their Estates after a reprize to the Cromwellian in possession. As there was no reprize to be had, Colonel Costello was rendered like so many more, desperate.

The year 1666 was expected, for some reason or other, to be an Annus Mirabilis, or year of wonders. A war was apprehended from France, and the tories were stirring all over Ireland.

Lieutenant Nangle, formerly of the Army, a Protestant, but now a proselyte to Rome, went into rebellion, and wandering (to use Ormonde's expression) from his debts and his wits, was finally shot dead in an attack on Lord Aungier's Castle at Longford. He and Costello joined forces, the one a more considerable man than the other. Ormonde mentioning the occurrence to Lord Chancellor Clarendon, calls Dudley Costello " a tall fellow, that was in Flanders when you and I were there."

Nangle and Costello were driven out of Connaught into Ulster. Sir Mathew Appleyard, Governor of Charlemont Fort, reported to the Duke of Ormonde (June, 1666), that with Lord Charlemont's troop and some foot and dragoons, he had marched to Dungannon,

and thence with the horse to Fintona before the sun
was up, in hopes to surprise Nangle and Costello. They
had all been drinking in an old Scotchman's house in
Fintona, when the market people and a scout they had
abroad, called upon them to fly, for the troops were
coming. Colonel Costello was now driven back into
Connaught, and proclaimed a tory and rebel. Lord
Dillon of Costello seems to have had some pity for
him, and wrote him two letters entreating him to come
in and surrender. But Colonel Dudley Costello knew
too well the terms that would be required. As for
Dud Costello (writes Ormonde to Lord Dillon, 7th July,
1666), unless he will undertake to bring to justice some
of his fellows, especially one Hill and one Plunket, who
lately committed some outrages in the north, and are
since come into Connaught,—if he can draw these men
into a trap, and deliver them to justice, I will undertake
his pardon, but on no other terms. These terms he
scorned. And furious at being " proclaimed," he
wrote the following defiant letter to Lord Dillon :

" Gortlaghane,
" The 18th of August, 1666.

" My Lord,—My being proclaimed traitor without
questioning or summoning me to my vindication, is so
base a practice that a man of honour would die
sooner . . . . Now that they (the informers)
have acted their part of the tragedy, it is time I should
come and act mine, which I intend in another guised
manner than they acted theirs,—they going under a
mask, I walking in my own colours . . . . and
making use of no actors but such as will openly
own it.

" My Lord, I have so much of honour yet left me

(which my adversaries know very well, though they will not own it), that I will not, unawares, seek their destruction as they did mine, but do declare by these presents that I will by killing, and by burning both corn and houses, act my part in their destructive tragedy. Let them prevent it the best way they may, now that they have timely notice. If they had dealt thus generously with me, I would have prevented their design of having me proclaimed traitor by the vindication of my innocence of what was laid to my charge."

He charges Lord Dillon's kinsmen with being the enemies that had done him this dis-service, and addresses Lord Dillon that he may inform them of his purpose.

" I understand, my Lord (he concludes), though you had not a hand hitherto in the matter, your Lordship approves very much of the act (of his being outlawed), and that withal you threaten a general destruction to both those baronies of yours (Costello and Gallen) for their relation to me. If you really intend it, your Lordship cannot fix upon a more fitting instrument or a man that will be humbler and more fitting to effect it than, my Lord,

" Your Lordship's most obedient servant,

" DUDLEY COSTELLO.

" For the Right Hon. the Lord Viscount
" Dillon of Costello, These."[1]

Shortly after this, Lord Dillon, having gone up to Dublin, Dudley Costello, with seventeen or eighteen lusty Kernes well armed, appeared and apprised Lord

[1] C. P. xxx., 26.

Dillon's tenants of the baronies of Costello and Gallen to quit, or he would burn both them and their corn together in autumn when in haggard.

Lord Kingston, President of Connaught, came himself in October to Boyle, and met Lord Dillon's steward, and urged that he should employ some of Lord Dillon's tenants to set Colonel Dudley Costello and betray him to his pursuers. His answer was that Colonel Costello was so beloved of the people that it was impossible. They had tried it; but the men intrusted had become *his* instead of their intelligencers.

Meanwhile Costello was not idle. Costello and his band of about thirty men (writes Captain Caulfeild to Lord Kingston, then at his residence of Mitchelstown Castle, Tipperary), some three hours before day on the 27th of November, burnt Castlemore, having entered by means of a turf stack placed against the bawn (or fortified curtilage), burnt Mr. Ormsby's house and barns; only the new tower, which was defended by two soldiers (the rest of the party being abroad with Sir Francis Gore), who killed two of the enemy, who thereupon marched away. And on Monday last they burned Ballylehane; since then they have done nothing.[1]

But on 26th December, Theobald Dillon wrote that Dudley Costello, ere yesternight, burnt three towns of his farm in Gallen, Tallemacorra, Tollanehan, and Fazyneys, and four villages in Costello, as part of Coylemorelorga, Tawnogna, and Arencagh, in the parish of Killeogh, and that he was resolved to burn

---

[1] Captain Thomas Caulfeild, Vice-President to John, Earl of Kingston, President of Connaught, dated Dunammon, 3rd December, 1666. C. P. xxxv., 105.

all those two baronies. Dillon's messenger gave out that he was three-score strong.

On 21st December, 1666, Lord Dillon wrote to Lord Kingston from Lough Glin, that on his arrival there, he found that Dudley Costello, the night but one before, had burnt the villages of Killmoore, Ardehville, and Coyle Cashel ; and last night was burning each side of the Moy, about Loughmackerkan and New-castle, and intended to run that course through both baronies. And as soon as he had done burning, threatened to hough and hew their cattle.

Orrery, Lord President of Munster, a neighbour of Lord Kingston's, now appears upon the scene to furnish Lord Kingston with a Munster spy, who undertook " to bring in the head of that uncircumcised Philistine that had given Lord Dillon so much trouble in Connaught."

Lord Kingston writes to Ormonde, that so villainous was the aspect of this spy, that he thought it were not much difference whether he brought in Costello's head or Costello his !

But Costello was near his end. On 3rd March, 1667, Captain Theobald Dillon, finding that Dudley and his men were at Culecorny, on the other side of the Moy, marched thither.

He could get no intelligence of the rebels being near, and had dispersed his men into two little villages to eat, but he fortunately kept six or seven of his men together, who proved a *Courte de Garde.* For, between 7 and 8 o'clock, the rebels were upon them. After some dispute of shot, they took to the sword.

Walter Jordan, an old soldier of Dillon's, was killed, and others of them wounded. But Dillon, coming up with fifteen or sixteen fresh men, Dudley and the rebels being, as it seemed to Dillon, forty men, rallied together, and stood until Dillon and his men came within pistol shot. There the two first ranks of Dillon's men gave fire, and Dudley was shot stone dead, and all the rest routed,—some of them desperately wounded. Lord Dillon informing the Duke of Ormonde of this event, said that he had set up Dudley Costello's head on Castlemore. But Ormonde ordered it to be sent up to Dublin, where probably for many months it adorned the prison tower or the principal gate of Dublin Castle.

There is the following curious incidental proof of the great popularity of Colonel Dudley Costello. Major Edward Hamilton, a Scottish Royalist, who had fought under Montrose, and had mortgaged his estate till he had nothing left, sought some relief from the King.

He was accordingly recommended for some valuable appointment, and was made by Ormonde High Sheriff of the county of Galway, in the year 1664, believing that Major Hamilton would derive profit from executing the Decrees of the Court of Claims ; but the Court was too soon adjourned to Major Hamilton's great loss. Ormonde then appointed him collector of Excise in the counties of Galway, Mayo, and Roscommon. But his deputies taking advantage of the disturbances raised by Colonel Dudley Costello, fled away with the moneys collected, some to Colonel Costello,—some to the Barbadoes, and elsewhere, leaving Major Hamilton debtor to the Inland Exchequer in £450.

IN 1610 King James the First formed the Ulster plantation. The O'Neils, the O'Donels, the Maguires, the O'Quins, the O'Hagans, and other ancient Irish Septs who were wont to boast that they and their ancestors held their territories from before the birth of Christ, had to give way to strangers from Scotland and England, or to retired officers of the army or Civil Service, called Servitors, and to see their homes and land, the support of themselves and their families, divided before their faces among these interlopers.

When the civil war began between England and Scotland in 1639 and 1640, and gave the Irish hopes of success, the rebellion, as was natural, broke out in Ulster.

The 23rd of October, 1641, was the fatal day.

When the rebellion was subdued in 1652, Cromwell and the Parliament made short work with the claims of such of the Irish as James the First had given allotments to in baronies assigned to Natives. For that King boasted of his justice as well as statesmanship in not entirely stripping the Irish and driving out the owners with the rest of the natives, as Queen Elizabeth had done in the Munster plantation.

During the War against the Parliament there were none more steadfast in their support of the Nuncio than the Ulster Irish. They could not induce the Confed-

erate Catholics to make it a condition or article of the
Peace with the King, either in that of 1646, or of
1648, that the Ulster plantation should be reversed
and the natives of Ulster restored.  For that would
have alienated from the King's Cause the Scottish
Presbyterians, the Hamiltons and others, who, though
Covenanters, were royalists, and the Episcopalian
Scotch, like the Stewarts and Montgomeries.  At the
Restoration only three of the Ulster nobility and
gentry were restored, the Marquis of Antrim, one of
the Maginises, and Sir Henry O'Neill of Shane's
Castle ; and these not in the Ulster plantation, but in
Down and Antrim.

" It is with tears in my eyes I say it (said Primate
Plunket, 13th May, 1671,) that in all Ulster there are
scarcely three gentlemen who have got back their lands
that were seized by Cromwell.[1]

" All the others (he adds) must ask as a favour to
farm small scraps of their former estates—and a great
favour it is when this is granted.[2]

" It was really pitiable (he said) to see high families
of the houses of O'Neil, O'Donel, Maguire, MacMahon,
Maginnis, O'Cahan, O'Kelly, O'Ferrall, who were great
princes in the memory of his (the Primate's) father,
and of many yet living, so reduced that they were
without property and without maintenance or means of
education for their sons and daughters."[3]

And he describes Dr. Patrick Plunket, Bishop of
Meath, giving private charity to gentlemen reduced

---

[1] Pp. 107, 114.  Memoirs of the Most Rev. Oliver Plunket, Archbishop
and Primate, by the Very Rev. Patrick Moran, D.D., Archbishop and Primate.  8vo.  James Duffy and Sons, Dublin.  1861.

[2] Ibid.

[3] Ibid., p. 110.

from good estate to poverty, ashamed to beg, and to widows, then in large numbers, through the massacre of Cromwell.[1]

The farmers were better off, and gave relief to those they were once the dependents of.[2]

In almost every diocese of the Province of Armagh except Meath, where many of the old Lords of the English Pale had been restored, no Catholic had any landed property, but were, except two or three in a few dioceses, tenants under Protestant or Presbyterian landlords.[3]

Many of the Irish gentry reduced to desperation through poverty joined the tories, and were outlawed. Primate Plunket sought them out in woods and mountains, and by his persuasions induced them to submit, and not only obtained their pardon, but the pardon of those that harboured or received them, and thus freed hundreds and hundreds of Catholic families from danger to their lives and properties. The gentry then embarked for France or Spain.[4]

For this he incurred the hostility of the tories. Led on, or set on, by a friar who consorted with them, a band of them attacked his house at midnight, held a sword at his throat, and robbed him of all the little money that he had in the house.[5]

The Primate incurred the hostility of some of the Franciscans in another way. He found them dwelling

---

[1] P. 161. Memoirs of the Most Rev. Oliver Plunket, Archbishop and Primate, by the Very Rev. Patrick Moran, D.D. 8vo. James Duffy and Sons, Dublin. 1861.
[2] Ibid., 108.
[3] Ibid., 149.
[4] Ibid., 57.
[5] Ibid., 283.

as private chaplains in the mansions of such of the
Catholic nobility and gentry as had recovered their
properties.   Instead of going their journeys on foot,
as they were required by the rule of their Order, and
as they did in Germany and the Low Countries, there
was scarce one of them but rode on horseback,
attended by a groom.   They dressed in superfine cloth
with French hat, and cravat bordered with lace, while
many of the Irish gentry, reduced to poverty, tra-
velled on foot clad in Louth frize,[1] worth two shillings
a yard.[2]

The Primate endeavoured also to bring the Franciscans all to live in convents, and to give up entertaining
as their guests at table gentlemen and even their
wives.[3]

But Primate Plunket was incurring other risks in
his endeavours to help the despoiled gentry who had
joined the tories to quit that course of life.   In the
Earl of Essex's time, " the Great Tory Fleming,"
(perhaps one of the Flemings of the Lord Slane's
family,) had done great harms with his band of tories.
Primate Plunket dealt with the Earl of Essex, then
Lord Lieutenant, for a licence for Fleming to quit the
kingdom, and communicated with Fleming using his
(the Primate's) assumed name of Cox.   It marks the
strangeness of the time that Fleming was introduced
to the Earl of Essex by Chief Baron Hen.   Through
some mischance the treaty miscarried.   For, instead
of quitting the kingdom, Fleming and some of his
associates was killed in February, 1678, "and thus

---

[1] Ibid., 81.
[2] Ibid., 64.
[3] Ibid.

(said Ormonde,) a good end was put to that negociation." But in the pocket of Fleming was found the
Primate's letter with the assumed name of Cox; and
afterwards the letter was endeavoured to be used as
evidence against the Primate while he was a prisoner
in London for the alleged Popish Plot. But Ormonde
showed the innocence of the Primate in regard to the
letter as above detailed.[1]

But there still remained many bands of tories in the
secluded parts of Ulster after all the efforts of Primate
Plunket. What then was their resource? First, the
charity of their former tenants and dependants,—for
hospitality and sympathy are the heavenly virtues of
the Irish. Next, some occasional relief from a more
fortunate kinsman or friend, whose small estate might
have escaped the eye of the Cromwellian soldiery,—a
not unknown occurrence, as appeared by the many
" discoveries" made after the Restoration.

The last resource—should he not have been able or
willing to take some small portion of his ancient lands
to farm under the new proprietor—was, levies from the
Adventurer or Officer in possession to support the old
proprietor, his wife and children. This was effected
by a regular circular notice, describing the necessity
he was under of marrying a daughter or sending a son
beyond sea. Or some of his old dependants, tories of
the neighbourhood, sympathizing with their former
master and his distressed family, seized the usurping
stranger's cows, or boldly robbed upon the highway,
and thus provided for him, and for themselves, too.

---

[1] Ormonde to the Earl of Sunderland, Dublin, 20th November, 1680,
C. P. cxlvi., 303.

Thus, on the 29th of April, 1670, we find the Lord Lieutenant (Lord Berkeley) and Council addressing Viscount Charlemont at Castle-Caulfield, in the county of Tyrone, informing him, that they were given to understand that some of the sept of the O'Neils, and others in that province [of Ulster] who had no visible means of subsistence, did yet live at a very high rate ; some of their sons being in rebellion ; from whom, by the spoil of His Majesty's good subjects, their parents had their support.    And such, and so great was the boldness of divers rebells in those parts, that they presumed to send their ticquetts or notes to some of His Majesty's good subjects in those parts, requiring them to send to the parents or friends of those rebels, for helpes in corn or cattle towards the marriage of their daughters or other relations—which the poor people dared not oppose, for fear of having their houses burnt, and other mischiefs done them by those rebels.    And for as much as those offences were of a transcendant nature, and might not be lightly passed over without exemplary punishment, and so His Majesty's good subjects freed from such apprehensions, Lord Charlemont was to examine what persons had presumed to offend in any of those kinds, and to endeavour the apprehension of such offenders and their parents, when His Excellency and the Council would give such further orders as the case should require.    From the Council Chamber in Dublin, 29th April, 1670.[1]

But it sometimes happened that those whose humanity had got the better of their national principles were dealt with by the State as the offenders.    Thus,

---

[1] See the original, Domestic Correspondence, 1668. (Council Book), p. 72, preserved in the State Paper Office, Dublin Castle.

on the 27th May, 1675, Symon Richardson, Francis Richardson, Henry Richardson, and Francis Lucas, Esquires (probably of the family of the Richardsons, then and now settled at Rich Hill, in the county of Armagh), were summoned to appear before the Lord Lieutenant and Council in person, on the 7th June, to answer a complaint preferred against them for harbouring some tories that lately robbed Mr. King. And there was a little postscript, of some significance, to Sir William Davys's summons, to the following effect :—
" It is also His Excellency's pleasure that Mr. Francis Lucas's wife, together with Miss Mary Brookes, do appear as above."[1]

For it will appear, when we come to the history of Redmond O'Hanlon, that the sympathies of the gentler sex were sometimes engaged on behalf of the tories. And we shall find no less a person than Deborah Annesley, the daughter of Henry Jones, Bishop of Meath (formerly Scout Master General to Cromwell), holding correspondence with that gallant outlaw, and concerting measures with him to preserve his life. All kinds of unworthy motives were of course attributed to any gentlemen who complied with these poor tories ; but there can be little doubt that they felt for their sad condition, and remembered that they themselves were in possession of their lands and livings.

Ulster was their chief seat. The passing of the Act of Explanation on 24th December, 1665, which shut the door of hope on almost all the Irish, caused the deepest discontent and despair—particularly amongst the native gentry of Ulster, who continued to claim the

---

[1] Domestic Correspondence, 1668. (Council Book), p. 72, Record Tower, Dublin Castle.

relics of their estates left with them by King James
the First after the plantation of Ulster, which they had
still hoped to be established in by the Court of
Claims.[1]   The war with the Dutch occurring at this
time inspired them with hopes, and from 1666 to 1690,
the Government and the British Planters were kept in
continual alarm.

For, contrary to the received opinion, Ulster
continued to be the dangerous part of Ireland till after
the War of the Revolution, when it was nearly colonized
anew by the Scotch suttlers and camp-followers of King
William's foreign forces. Eighty thousand small Scotch
Adventurers came in between 1690 and 1698, into
different parts of Ireland, but chiefly into Ulster.

On March the 4th, 1666, writes an intelligencer of
Sir Richard Kennedy, one of the Barons of the Exchequer : "In Londonderry and Tyrone I had the company
of several of the Irish gentry, whom I found in general
unsatisfied with the passing of the Bill [of Explanation],
and espetially the O'Neils and O'Reillys, M'Mahons
and Maguires, and the O'Donnels and O'Kanes . . . .
and there are a considerable number of young gentlemen
of those families much in despair, and in their discourse

---

[1] "There was not above three or four Roman Catholics of Ulster restored
to their estates, which were of the Marquis of Antrim, Sir Henry O'Neil,
M'Gennis, with one more.  And, yet, when Owen O'Neil relieved the Cootes
in Derry (A.D. 1649), to yᵉ destruction of the King's interest in Ireland ; at
that very time four Colonels quitted their rebellious General O'Neil, and
brought their Regiments to Ormond, viz. : the Lord Iveagh (pronounced
Evagh), Colonel O'Neil, of the Fews, Colonel M'Mahon, and Colonel
O'Reilly. None of these, nor any under their command, got one foot of their
estates, and yet the family of the Cootes were advanced to great honours."
Collections by friends, some of us eye-witnesses of the warr and rebellion in
Ireland since 1641.   Preserved amongst the Carte Papers, vol. lxiv.,
p. 431.

very bitter against the proceedings of this Parliament. . . . ."[1]

At this period " the condition of the most part of
Ulster " (to use the words of Sir George Acheson,
ancestor of the present Earl Gosford), " was such as
none dare travel or inhabit there, but as in an enemy's
country ; no trade, no work, no improvement ; all
which he attributed to the tories. They were against
all industry and improvement, as tending to bring in
British to extrude them. So that it was held a point
of gallantry to turn tories, and all their discourses and
songs were in their praise, and they accounted heroes.
The embarrassed English gentry had them for dependants and purveyors—the common English, living
abroad in detached houses, feared them.

Formerly they robbed, and went upon their keeping ;
then they were in armed bands and they forced most
part of the British to pay them yearly contributions,
"in paying of which, if they be negligent or not punctual,
they presently come, rob their houses, drive away their
cattle into their retreats ; that is, those mountainous
and boggy and coarse lands inhabited only by natives,
whereof there are many in Ulster, and here they detain
them till they pay much more than was at first
demanded. This new way of torying was first brought
in among them, and shown them by such as had been
abroad to forraigne warrs, . . . the like practices
being too much used abroad, and permitted the soldiery
by military connivance."

One great encouragement of toryism was, " the
foolish ancient way of hospitality to receive and give

---

[1] "N. D." to Sir Richard Kennedy.   Carte Papers, vol. xxxiv.,
p. 390.

food to all comers of their nation, not inquiring the cause of their coming or business ; so that they continue wandering about from house to house as long as they will, . . . alledging themselves Innocents, but necessitated so to do, having not wherewithal to pay the fees of their tryall and acquittal in the Court of Claims.

" One design of these men is," says Sir George Acheson, " that thus terrifying and discouraging the British, having nothing certain, but all at their mercy, they will induce them by degrees to leave those places of danger and recede into those more secure, which they daily begin now to do ; and so the lands will be laid waste, none else daring to take them, whereby the natives will rent them at such mean values as they please, and thereby embody themselves, and grow numerous and opulent."

Sir George Acheson's remedy was a truly military kind of justice. An officer with a " volant [or flying] party" of troopers was to be established, with liberty to call upon any man to stand in the King's name, and give an account of himself, and to shoot him if he didn't ; if he did, to try him by a jury on the spot, and, if guilty, " to proceed to sentence, and (after Christian preparation), to hang him." In which circumstances many a man would rather stand his chance of a volley from the troopers than a verdict of the jurors.[1]

It is quite plain, however, from the various engagements which the Lord Lieutenant and Council entered into with tories all over the kingdom—for killing each other, or for abjuring the realm, or for pardon and

[1] " The Tories of Ulster," by Sir George Acheson, Knt..and Bart. [1667]. Carte Papers, Bodleian Library, vol. xlv., p. 309.

liberty to stay in it on condition of driving out other tories within a given time—that Sir George Acheson's scheme had every recommendation but practicability. The tories were, in fact, too numerous, and the forces at the disposal of the Government too few to cope with them in the wild and difficult countries then frequent in Ireland.

Lord Charlemont, in like manner, in October, 1668, by direction from the Earl of Ossory, then Lord Deputy, and the Council, was directed to send for "two Ulster tories, namely, Neile Oge O'Neile and Con his brother, sonnes unto Tirlagh M'Shane Oge O'Neile,"[1] and if, upon conference with them at Castle Caulfield (his residence in the county of Tyrone), he should find that they might be willing, on promise of their own pardon, to do service against the tories that were abroad upon their keeping, the Board authorized him to give them protection for such time as he thought necessary, not exceeding six months.[2]

But they, either from inability or unwillingness, seemed to have failed in their undertaking, and to have forfeited their protection ; for just eighteen months afterwards (May 17, 1670), Lord Berkeley (Lord Lieutenant) and the Council are again in communication with Lord Charlemont. Considering (they said) how the provinces of Ulster and Connaught were then infested by tories ; and that it appeared from Captain Golborne's letter to Lord Charlemont that Con O'Neile offered to give security to clear both provinces of all the tories, and either to kill, take, or drive

---

[1] This only means Terence, son of John O'Neile the younger.

[2] Council Book. Domestic Correspondence, 1668, fol. 44, Record Tower, Dublin Castle.

them out of the kingdom; and as Lord Charlemont
had written that Con and his brother Neile were the
most likely persons to perform what they promised, if
they might have their pardon, and remain still in the
realm, the Lord Lieutenant and Council authorized him
to engage with them on these terms—provided that,
before the 1st of August following, they cleared Ulster
and Connaught of all the tories.[1]

For some reason or other this negotiation did not
succeed—for, their father endeavoured, in his conference with Lord Charlemont, to stipulate for the return
from exile of them and his nephews, as appears from
this—that on the 1st June, 1670, the Lord Lieutenant
and Council apprise Lord Charlemont that "they had
considered of the proposal presented by him at the
Board, from Captain Tirlagh M'Shane Oge O'Neile, in
behalf of his three sons, Neile O'Neile, Con O'Neile,
and Owen O'Neile, and his two nephews, Brian
O'Cahan and Shane O'Neile; and they conceived that
the same Captain Tirlagh M'Shane O'Neile, Oge
O'Neile, and his friends and relations might, if they
pleased, without the presence or assistance of his said
sons and nephews (whom he desired should be
recalled from their alledged banishment), performe the
services which he proposed. They therefore authorized Lord Charlemont to say, that if he should, before
the 1st August [1670] kill, take, or drive out the
tories, then they would allow his sons and nephews to
return—they giving good securities for their peaceable
conduct. [2]

---

[1] Council Book. Domestic Correspondence, 16f8, fol. 75.
[2] Ibid.

At this time Lord Charlemont was Governor of
Ulster, and it was his duty to pay the head money
offered by proclamation for the heads of tories hunted
and slain. Thus, on 29th August, 1670, the Lord
Lieutenant and Council, by letters of concordatum,
repaid twenty pounds paid by him to Captain James
Stuart and his party, on the certificate of Michael
Cole, Esq., Sheriff of the county of Fermanagh, that
the said captain and his party, on the 4th of July previous, at Coolaghtie, in the said county, killed and
beheaded one Owen M'Guire, a notorious rebel and
tory (whose name was inserted in the proclamation of
the Council Board of 1st June, 1670), and had
brought his head to the Sheriff, which was put up at
Inniskillen pursuant to the proclamation.[1] On 25th
November, 1670, he was repaid a like sum, paid to
Bernard Butterfield, Esq., on the certificate of Alexander M'Causland, Esq., Sheriff of the county of
Tyrone, who, on the 18th of July previous, went forth
with a party in pursuit of several tories, and at a place
called Evisegodan, in the said county, did there kill
and behead one Patrick O'Sonnaghan, a notorious rebel
and tory, included in the same proclamation.[2] Among
many similar letters of concordatum, for repayments of
head money to Lord Charlemont, there is one in favour
of Mulmurry O'Hossa, dated 25th November, 1670.

Mulmurry O'Hossa describes himself, in his petition
to the Lord Lieutenant and Council, as once a lieutenant in the regiment of H. R. H. the Duke of York,
in Flanders ; and states that, in pursuance of the late

---

[1] Records of the Vice-Treasurer's Office, now preserved in the Custom
House Buildings, Dublin.

[2] Ibid.

proclamation, and by the special encouragement of William Archdall, Esq., one of His Majesty's Justices of the Peace for the county of Fermanagh, he had then of late pursued and slain two notorious tories, called Daniel O'Roarty and James O'Loughnane, who, by their frequent robberies, did very much infest and molest His Majesty's good subjects in Fermanagh and the several adjacent counties ; " the heads of which said tories your Petitioner brought, in open court, before the Justices of the Peace, at a General Sessions held at Inniskillen, and the said heads, set up, are still remaining in the said county town of Inniskillen. Since which time the brother of the said Roarty is run out into the company of Edmund M'Gillaspie, Hugh M'Nelagh, and other notorious toryes in the proclamation, and came several times to kill your Petitioner."

Unable to get any satisfaction for this service from Lord Charlemont, Governor of Ulster, " in regard the said tories killed, were not inserted in the proclamation (though they were of the company of Owen M'Guire and John Magragh, who were proclaimed tories, and the next day after pursued and killed by Captain Hassett and Captain Stuart)," Mulmurry O'Hossa had been obliged to make a journey purposely to this city of Dublin, where he then attended with great expense, above his weak ability, seeking the reward of twenty pounds per head.   He supports his claim on the certificate of Michael Cole, Esq., the Sheriff, and the Justices.   The latter certificate runs thus :—

"Co. Fermanagh, } At a General Sessions of the Peace,
              } held at Inniskillen, for the said Co.
*to wit.*     } of Fermanagh, the 5th of July, 1670.

"These are to certifie that one Mulmurry O'Hossa, Gent., att the said Sessions, in open court, brought in before William Archdall, Abraham Creightoune, Gerald Irvine, and John Creightoune, Esqs., four of His Majesty's Justices of the Peace in the said county, the heads of Donel O'Rortie, late of the county of Donegal, yeoman, and James O'Loughnane, late of the county of Tirone, yeoman ; which said persons have been made appear unto us, by oath of several persons, to be notorious rebels, and have been guilty of several robberies and other misdemeanours, and were killed by the aforesaid Mulmurry O'Hossa, Gent., at Strana-darrow, in the county of Fermanagh aforesaid, the 5th July, 1670.

WILLIAM ARCHDALL.
ABRA. CREIGHTOUNE.
GER. IRVINE.
JOHN CREIGHTOUNE."[1]

From the Sheriff's certificate, it appears that these two tories were killed on the 5th of July ; so that Lieutenant Mulmurry O'Hossa must have hastened to present their heads, all dripping with fresh gore, to the magistrates assembled at Sessions in Inniskillen—a dainty dish, truly, to set before a Bench. It is satisfactory to know that the Lord Lieutenant and Council recognized Lieutenant Mulmurry O'Hossa's zeal and intelligence, and that he was not disappointed of his forty pieces of silver (or gold).

---

[1] Records of the Vice-Treasurer's Office, Custom House Buildings, Dublin.

Such engagements as these were evidently of little avail; for we find Lord Charlemont and others constantly employed by the Lord Lieutenant and Council in treaties with tories to abjure the realm. On the 18th of March, 1670, he was instructed to parley with Edmund Gillespie and Redmond M'Knogher M'Quoid, and to take security that they would depart the kingdom within three months, never to return.[1] On the 28th of the same month he was authorized to make a similar arrangement with Rory M'Donnel, Owen Duff M'Donnel, Fardorogh M'Donnel, Toole M'Donnell, and Shane M'Grath.

It was against his will, however, that the Duke of Ormonde entered into agreements with the tories for abjuring the realm; for to give them leave after all their robberies and depredations to quit the kingdom was, he feared, to encourage the trade, and raise more than should be sent away.

" For who (he asks) in the condition many of the Irish are would not, by robbing and spoyling, gather a summe of money to transport himself beyond sea, to get a fortune of which he despairs in his own country; especially not being restrained by any principles of conscience or of kindness to those they destroy ; and perhaps being told by their spiritual misleaders that the course they are in is little worse than spoyling the Egyptians was in the Israelites? The course your Lordship has taken [he concludes this letter, to Colonel Mark Trevor, Lord Dungannon, Governor of Ulster] of setting distrust and enmity betwixt themselves is certainly the best, and ought not only to be pursued but encouraged, by giving such as perform their

[1] Council Book, Domestic Correspondence, 1668, folio 69, preserved in the Record Tower, Dublin Castle.

undertakings faithfully some reward beyond pardon."[1]

One of the most active tory hunters in Ulster was Captain William Hamilton, who, in 1682, commanded a troop of dragoons in the Earl of Arran's regiment of Horse. He had a warrant or commission from the Duke of Ormonde for the purpose of killing or treating with them as he thought best. Sir William Stewart, writing to Ormonde, from Newtown Stewart, says, never was there a fitter man for the employment that Ormonde had given him than young Captain Hamilton. He had a few days before killed two or three of them. He never let them rest nor rested himself from following them. If ever there was perpetual motion it was his.[2] His praises were sung also by Sir William Stewart of Ramelton, Viscount Mountjoy. A band of tories, horse and foot, that lately gathered in the county of Down, had given Captain Hamilton and his dragoons (he said) some diversion. "Last week he sent an account (continues Lord Mountjoy) of having destroyed two of the chief of them, and I believe will very soon despatch the rest. Scanderbeg (adds Lord Mountjoy) was not a greater scourge to the Turks than this Scabberhead is to tories,· nor did he kill more with his own hand."

But the best swimmers come short home at last !

Soon after Lord Mountjoy's praises, Captain W. Hamilton fell a victim to the tories he was following. There remains no detailed account of the occurrence, but from some expressions used by Ormonde it would

[1] Carte Papers, vol. xlix., last page.
[2] December 15, 1682. C. P. ccxvi., 122.

seem as if he had met his fate through mismanage-
ment arising from some hostility between those in
command on the occasion.

Chief Justice Keatinge had just returned from the
Kilkenny assizes (Summer 1686), and had described
the generation or coherency of robbery, theft, and
perjury, crimes that, Ormonde said in his answer to the
Chief Justice, were more prevalent in Ireland, he
thought, than in any other part of the world. And he
quite approved of the Chief Justice's generation of
these crimes.

Thefts begat outlawry, and that jail breaking; jail
breaking begat " running out and being on their keeping " (as it was called), which improved into torying,
or rebellion in little. That produced malice against
the prosecutors of it, and propagated perjury ; " and
thus came poor Will to his end." The Chief Justice
had, evidently, not heard when he wrote (said Ormonde), of the " murther of Captain Wm. Hamilton,
at Downpatrick, for so it was called in his (Ormonde's)
letters; but (he continued), whatever should prove the
occasion of it, it might well be attributed to one or all
of the above mentioned crimes."

It was perhaps one of these tories of whom the
following tale is told in a letter to Ormonde's Secretary :—

" Here is little worth mention (said Gerard Borr to
Henry Gascoigne) beyond an odd accident that lately
happened at Downpatrick. Three grand tories having
been this assizes condemned there for robbery, the
jailer, executioner, &c., went into the jail at the time

---

[1] Ormonde to Lord Chief Justice Keatinge, St. James's Square, London,
August 12th, 1686. C. P. 243.

appointed to bring forth the prisoners to execution, and the executioner offering to put a halter round Doran's neck (one of the three) who had a *skeine*, or *madogue*, privately conveyed to him that morning by his wife, he therewith stabbed the hangman to the heart, who fell dead on the spot, and wounded the jailer and two more before they could get the *skeine* out of his hand. This so terrified the executioners of that country, that none of the trade would venture on these toryes, which forced the Sheriff to deal (by pro-mise of a reprieve), with one of the three, to hang his two comrades, whereof Doran one, which a Judge has since granted, and I believe the new executioner will have the favour to be transported."[1]

Chief among the tories of the counties of Down, Armagh, and Tyrone, was Redmond O'Hanlon. His principal haunt was the Fews Mountains, overhanging Newry. Thence his retreat was easy to the neighbour-ing mountains of Mourne, on the north side of the bay of Carlingford. For more than ten years he kept three counties in subjection ; so that none dared travel with-out convoy, or his pass. The other tories were under him. One of them, Cormac O'Murphy, weary to be under Redmond O'Hanlon, set up for himself, became a ringleader of a company of his own, and plundered three Scotchmen, who were tributaries to Redmond O'Hanlon, it being a custom for the country people in Ireland to pay the tories for a pass to go unmolested. These Scotchmen complained to Redmond O'Hanlon, who trepanned O'Murphy, under pretence he wanted his aid to take a booty. When he appeared, he ordered

[1] Gerard Borr (Secretary to the Earl of Arran) to Henry Gascoigne (Secretary to the Duke of Ormonde), 24th April, 1885. C. P. ccxvii., 68.

his men to disarm him, and send him to the Scotchmen, with a guard of fourteen tories, and a Mittimus from Redmond to the next magistrate. But the Scotchmen compounded the matter with Cormac O'Murphy for £20, to be paid the week following.

Cormac, being thus set at liberty, got new arms, and sent a challenge to Redmond O'Hanlon, who refused to appear, but swore he would be revenged on Cormac. Edmund Murphy, parish priest of Killevy, titular Chanter of Armagh, living in the Fews, at the instigation of Captain Butler, who lay at Dundalk, at the foot of the mountains, with his company of foot (charged by the Duke of Ormonde with the following of Redmond O'Hanlon), plotted with Cormac O'Murphy to seize O'Hanlon. The first attempt was made by occasion of Cormac O'Murphy's surprising David Mulligan, of Lecorry, in the county of Armagh, and bidding him stand and deliver ; whereupon David Mulligan showed a pass from Redmond O'Hanlon, stating that David Mulligan and his father-in-law had often sheltered him when hard hunted by Sir Hans Hamilton. But Cormac, to enrage Redmond O'Hanlon, and show his contempt of him, refused to acknowledge his pass, and robbed David Mulligan, saying that he would only restore him the goods on Redmond's restoring him his arms. A meeting was appointed for the purpose of a mutual restoration, at which O'Hanlon was to be seized. The priest was to provide brandy and hot waters (not hot water), and Captain Butler, soldiers ; but this failed by David Mulligan's seizing Patrick Murphy, Cormac Murphy's " brother " and " kindred " under the Tory Acts, who, by this means, got back his goods; and thereupon Redmond O'Hanlon, finding that his friend had recovered his goods, refused to attend the meeting, and sent word to Cormac that he would not return him his arms. Another plot between the priest and Cormac O'Murphy for his capture was arranged on a similar plan. Cormac on one occasion robbed a cousin of O'Hanlon's, who, boasting that he had the protection of the chief rebels of the kingdom, and particularly one of O'Hanlon's passes, engaged to take some trader's goods under his charge to Dublin. Cormac was sure that Redmond O'Hanlon and his men would resent this outrage upon his authority, and would soon be after him. So he and the priest arranged another ambush, and informed Captain Butler, who had his men at hand ; but Redmond disappointed these and a thousand other schemes.

For these are only the contrivances (detailed by himself) of one priest whom he had outraged by threatening that he would make any one that went to listen to his preachings against him pay for the first offence, one cow ; for the second, two cows (which he put into execution against one of Edmund Murphy's parishioners) ; and for the third, death.[1]

Yet this man was a scholar and a gentleman, which is the reason Sir Francis Brewster assigns for his not being taken after committing so many robberies and murders as he debits him with.

His exploits appeared in the French Gazettes ; and by them he was called " Count O'Hanlon,"[2] which

---

[1] The above extracts are taken from the " Present State of Ireland, but more particularly of Ulster, represented to the People of England, by Edmund Murphy, Parish Priest, and Titular Chanter of Armagh, and one of the first discoverers of the Irish Plot." Folio, London, 1681.

[2] Carte's " Life of Ormonde," vol. ii., p. 812.

meant only that he was of gentle blood, and the son of an estated gentleman who had lost his property through the Court of Claims.

But Redmond's career, at the end of the year 1680, was drawing to a close.

In addition to the curious and voluminous details given by Father Murphy (of which what is given above is only a small fragment), we are accidentally in possession of the more dangerous practices of a Protestant Bishop against poor Redmond.

The year 1680 was the height of the calamitous and disgraceful popular frenzy in England of the sham Popish Plot. It became necessary, in support of the drama performing in England, to show that the Irish Papists were moving too, which could be easily done as regarded the tories, who would, no doubt, have accepted any aid, to reinvest them with their beloved homes and lands. But it should also be shown, for Shaftesbury's purposes, that the Popish priests were engaged in the plan of a French invasion of Ireland, and this must be kept in mind in reading the following correspondence. The first letter comes from Sir Hans Hamilton to Ormonde, dated December 18th, 1680.[1]

[1] " May it please your Grace.—About a fortnight ago, one, Owen Murphy, brought mee an order from your Grace and the Council, requiring all Officers, Civill and Military, to bee aiding and assisting to y⁰ said Murphy in apprehending and sending to Dublin all such persons as the said Murphy should thinke fitt to apprehend in order to the discovery of the Popish Plott in Ireland.

" Your Grace's most humble and
" obedient servantt,

" HANS HAMILTON.

" P.S.—These letters were found in the hands of Redmond O'Hanlon's mother-in-law, by one Mullen, whoe I employed to prosecute the toreys, and having apprehended some of Redmon's recevers in whose hands they found goods robbed from some travellers on the rode, the said woman was

Sir Hans (probably a Presbyterian) did not doubt, in his hatred of Prelacy, which he nearly couples with Popery, but that Henry Jones, Bishop of Meath, for a sum paid by Redmond O'Hanlon to Mr. Annesley, of Clough [Clough-Magheri-catt] in the county of Down, now Castlewellan, at the foot of the Mourne Mountains, was ready to obtain his pardon.

The letters that caused Sir Hans Hamilton's indignation was a correspondence of Mr. and Mrs. Annesley (the latter, Deborah Jones, daughter of the Bishop), with Katherine O'Hanlon, Redmond's mother-in-law, under the directions and authority of the Bishop. Her husband, Francis Annesley, was son of Sir Francis, first Viscount Valentia, ancestor of the present Earl Annesley.

The first letter is one from the Bishop, dated Dublin, Nov. 2, 1680, and begins :—" Deare Son and Daughter Annesley," and informs them that a proposal (on paper) of Hanlon's he had received from them, was read in the Privy Council that day ; and that his orders were to assure Hanlon of pardon on the terms formerly proposed, of his declaring himself, and assuring the Government of his reality, by first bringing in, or

in one of theire houses. Seeing Mullen come in, shee went to hide these letters. Hee believed it to bee money, went to her, and took them from her. The letters and the recovers hee brought to mee ; but not the woman. *And now your Grace sees that a small sum of money given to the sonne-in-law (for soe itt is probable to bee) will prevaile with that Bp. (bishop) to procure pardon for soe bloody murtherers as these are known to bee by one meanes or other.*

" Endorsed,
" S$^r$ Hans Hamilton.

Dat. 18 }
Rec. 20 } Dec. 1680.

Read at the Board, 20th Dec. 1680.
L$^{res}$ enclosed from y$^e$ Bishop of Meath.
—Carte Papers, vol. xxxix., p. 141.

H

cutting off some of the principal tories that were proclaimed : he and his friends afterwards performing
what they further undertook, viz. : to free the country
of tories.

The Bishop complains somewhat jealously of
O'Hanlon for dealing with the Bishop of Clogher when
he had begun with him, as appeared by the Primate's
reading a similar paper before the Council, that
O'Hanlon had sent to the Bishop of Clogher; but he
excuses it as probably caused by O'Hanlon's letter to
him, dated so long before as 30th September, having
only reached him the day before he read it at the
Council, and so remained unanswered.

An interval of a full month, fatal apparently to poor
Redmond O'Hanlon, elapsed between the foregoing
letter of the Bishop and the next addressed by his
daughter, Deborah Annesley, to " Mr. Hanlon,"
probably the father-in-law of Redmond. It is dated
December 7, 1680.[1]

She is extremely troubled that she cannot give
Redmond O'Hanlon ("Mr. O'Hanlon" she calls him)

---

[1] "*December* yᵉ 7th, 1680.

" Mr. Hanlon, I am extremely troubled, yᵗ I cannot give Mr. O'Hanlon
noe better account of what I was assured to prosper in.

"My Lᵈ. Lᵗ. was overruled by the Councell who would not heare of his
coming in, but has putt £200 on Redmon O'Hanlon, and £100 on loling
[Laughlin], so that yᵉ arguments could be use by my father could do noe
good. The Proclamation will be out a Saturday against them ; but my
father is finding out a way in England for al those pore men, of which you
shall know from Mr. Annesley : because Leters are opened, I can say no
more of that. But yᵗ way will, without doubt, secure them, and bring them
in, of which I desire you to sende away emediately to Mr. Annesley [who]
will desire to heare from you Concerning it ; and let them know yᵗ noe
menes shal be left unsought to doe them good, for my father will have them
in. And let them not take it eile [ill], for I [could] doe noe more if it had
bene for my own liife. I shal stay heare til I heare from you conserning
what I wrot about them to Mr. Annesley, and no ston shall be left unturned

no better account of what (in her gentle heart), she was assured to prosper in. The Lord Lieutenant was overruled by the Council, who would not hear of his coming in ; but had put £200 on Redmond, and £100 on Loughlin O'Hanlon ("Loling" she writes it), so that what arguments could be used by her father could do no good. "The proclamation," she adds, "will be out on Saturday ; but my father is finding out a way in England for al those pore men of which you shall know more from Mr. Annesley. . . . And let them not take it eile (ill), for I could doe noe more if it had bene for my owne liife." In a postscript this tender creature adds, "There is nothing sett on Edmond Bân [the fair] and Hagan."

Now, her father was engaged at that moment in helping the Earl of Shaftesbury to bring his tragedy of the sham Popish Plot, then playing in London, to a successful conclusion ; and the Bishop and his brother, Sir Theophilus Jones (made Scoutmaster-General for life in the Bishop's place at the Restoration), had sent over agents to London, to keep them in correspondence with Shaftesbury and the managers there.[1]

to bring them in, which I question not but we shal finde wil be wel con-serning them.

"I am, Sir,

"Your assured friend and Servant,

"DEB. ANNESLEY.

"There is nothing sett on Edmond Bân and Hagan."

—Carte Papers, vol. xxxix., p. 144.

[1] Part of Shaftesbury's design was to damage Ormonde. Ormonde's family were all Roman Catholics. Shaftesbury knew his fidelity to the King and dynasty. And he saw how difficult and dangerous a position Ormonde would be placed in, suspected by the English public of Popish sympathies.

The Earl of Arran, his son, and Lord Deputy, accordingly seized and secretly opened the Bishop's correspondence. His whole conduct is there-fore exhibited in the Carte Collection.

Throughout their whole lives these two brothers, sons of the "vivacious" (or long-lived) Bishop of Killaloe, who died aged 104, were deadly foes to the Irish. In May, 1652, Dr. Henry Jones, then Bishop of Clogher, and Scoutmaster-General, appeared at the Council of general and field officers of Ludlow's army, held at Kilkenny, and made the officers protest (through a dread only of the Lord, they trusted) against their General's too great aptness to mercy (so they termed it), and sparing those whom the Lord was pursuing with his great severity.[1]

From Cromwell[2] he obtained Lynch's Knock, the ancient estate of the Lynches, at Summerhill, in the county of Meath (now the noble demesne of the Lord Langford), as did Sir Theophilus the estate of the Sarsfields at Lucan. At the Restoration, Gerald Lynch sought to be restored. He had had two sons killed, fighting for the King under Ormonde, and a third followed the King's fortunes abroad, and there ended his days. He obtained His Majesty's Letters of the 30th of March, 1662, to be restored ; but the Bishop obtained a proviso in the Act of Settlement, confirming these lands to him, notwithstanding (as was urged by Sir Nicholas Plunket for Gerald Lynch) " the Bishop has a good bishoprick, while the said former proprietor and the rest of his children not

---

[1] Letter of the General and Field Officers, &c. to the Speaker of the House of Commons.—Books of the Lord Protector's Council of Ireland. $\frac{A}{90}$, p. 69, State Paper Office, Dublin Castle.

[2] Humble Petition of Dr. Henry Jones to the Right Hon. the Lord Deputy and Council, praying that Lynch's Knock and Jordanstown, now in his possession, may be passed to him by Patent, by name of the manor of Michael's Mount [1657].—MS. in Library of Trinity College, Dublin, F. 3. 18.

killed in your Majesty's service are in a sadd condition."[1]

The Bishop's purpose was to prove Archbishop
Plunket's complicity in a supposed French invasion.
Informers (particularly a degraded priest, the Edmund
Murphy mentioned above, and others), induced by
rewards and hopes of favour, swore that the Archbishop had made large levies of money from the priests
of his diocese to buy arms, and had surveyed the
neighbouring harbours, and had selected Carlingford
(a port with no depth of water, and where fishing
boats could scarce find access), as the place of disem-
barkation for 70,000 French soldiers. Whether the
Bishop, in his bigotry, believed in the truth of this
monstrous tale or not, Archbishop Plunket was
arrested, and sent for trial to London, the Bishop of
Meath alleging that his influence (the influence of
innocence and worth) was such in Ireland, there could
be no fair trial.[2]

To conclude with this poor Archbishop, he could
give no answer except a denial and statement of the
infamy of the witnesses, and protested that he could
fearlessly appeal to the Duke of Ormonde, the Earl of
Anglesey, and others of the best and highest Protestants in Ireland, if he were tried there ; or even if the
Court would wait for his witnesses who had already
arrived at Chester. As for the vast moneys collected,
he had never got so much out of them as to maintain
a servant, as was attested before the Council in Ire-

---

[1] "Schedule of Provisos in the late Act and draft of the present Bill
which relate to some not comprehended in your Majesty's Declaration, and
which do obstruct the performance of the ends thereof." Volumes relating
to the Act of Settlement. MS., Folio, State Paper Office, Dublin Castle.

[2] 2d Carte's " Life of Ormonde," p. 513, sect. 99.

land : he never had but one.  And the house he lived in was a little thatched house, wherein was only one little room for a library, which was but seven feet high.  However, all was vain, and he underwent the butchery allotted to treason, a victim for this sham Popish Plot, and French invasion, and Utopian Irish army of 70,000 men, (as he called it himself) at Tyburn, in 1681.[1]

The Bishop of Meath, being persuaded in his own mind that Redmond O'Hanlon must assuredly know everything about the designed invasion, hoped to get him for a witness against Archbishop Plunket, and to send him to London.

It is very possible that it was with the design of getting into the confidence and good will of Redmond O'Hanlon that he first employed his kind-hearted daughter to correspond with Redmond about his obtaining his pardon ; for,

> " —— no prayer, no moving art,
>   E'er bent that fierce inexorable heart."[2]

---

[1]  State Trials.

The Archbishop was held in high respect among the best of the Protestants in Ireland ; and it is a circumstance curiously illustrative of this estimation, that at a residence and school which he had established for Father Stephen Rice of the Society of Jesus in Drogheda (then and long after the seat of both the Protestant and Roman Catholic Primates), out of 150 pupils there were 40 of them Protestants.  "In the school," writes the Archbishop to Father Oliva, General of the Society of Jesus at Rome, "there are 150 boys, for the greater part children of the Catholic nobility and gentry, and there are also about 40 children of the Protestant gentry.  You may imagine (he adds) what envy it excites in the Protestant Masters and Ministers to see Protestant children coming to the schools of the Society. . . . Dublin, 22nd November, 1672."—Memoirs of the Most Rev. Oliver Plunket, Archbishop of Armagh and Primate of All Ireland, by His Eminence Cardinal Moran, Archbishop of Sydney, p. 100.  8vo.  Dublin, James Duffy and Sons, 1861—a work full of interest, and containing original historical documents of great value.

[2]  This Doctor Henry Jones it was that inflamed the officers of the English

It therefore may be that he only amused his daughter by stories of opposing the proclaiming of Redmond O'Hanlon ; and he may himself have planned it, as a means of driving him more certainly into his net.

Mr. Annesley's letter was of the same date and tenor as his wife's. He was directed, he says, " from above," to apprise Redmond O'Hanlon that £200 was set on his head, and that £100 was the price of the others.

" A pardon had certainly been obtained for you," he says, " if in so enormous a case it could have been done without violence to justice. I can tell you (if you come over to me, and possibly it may be worth your while) where the shoe pinches."

He then plainly requires to know if O'Hanlon will be a discoverer of the design for the French invasion here, and who in Ireland are the principal abettors.

---

army under Ludlow to frenzy against men who had nothing to say to the alleged crimes, even if true.

" Mr. Speaker, upon the 17th of April last many of your servants came into Kilkenny, and had a meeting with sundry of your generals and field officers. . . . . The observance of our General's aptness to mercy and to a composure with the enemy . . . . doth (through dread of the Lord only, we trust) occasion much remorce . . . . in most minds here concerning some treaties which are liable to be attended with sparing whom the Lord is pursuing with His great displeasure ; and whether our patient attending rather His further severity upon them be not most safe. *And whilst we were in debate hereof,* and of dealing with those that yet continue in rebellion, *an abstract of some particular murders was produced by the Scout Master-General* (who had the original examinations of them more at large) . . . . And indeed, so deeply were all affected with the barbarous wickedness of the actors in these cruel murthers and massacres . . . . that we are much afraid our behaviour towards this people may never sufficiently avenge the same . . . . And lest some tender concessions might be concluded through your unacquaintedness with these abominations, we have caused this enclosed abstract to be transcribed and made fit for your use. Kilkenny, May 5, 1652." ᴬ⁄₇₀ p. 69, " Books of the Council for the Affairs of Ireland." Record Tower, Dublin Castle.

In that case a pardon will be obtained.[1]    But O'Hanlon must have spurned the vile proposal, for during
six months more he lived, with £200 upon his head,
unkilled, uncaught, amongst the rocks of Slieve
Gullion, in the recesses of the Moyry Pass, or
amongst the broken hills around Forkhill ; for when,
instead of fearing or hating a man, the people *fear for
him*, he sees with many eyes, and hears with many
ears.    Though great attempts were made (says Sir
Francis Brewster), and large rewards offered for bringing in his head, both in the Earl of Essex's Lord Lieutenancy and the then present one, the army being put
to more trouble in attending and pursuing him and his
party than all the tories in the kingdom since the
general rebellion of Ireland, it was all in vain.    But
the Duke of Ormonde took at last his own way,
seeming quiet, and giving the Count no disturbance.
And that there should be no taking air of his design,
the Duke drew a commission and instructions all with
his own hand for two gentlemen he employed.    And
these were so well pursued by the gentlemen entrusted,
that on Monday, the 25th of April, 1681, at two in the
afternoon, Count Hanlon was shot through the heart.
" Thus fell this Irish Scanderbeg," concludes Sir Francis Brewster's letter, " who, considering the circumstances he lay under, and the short time he continued
to act, did things more to be admired than Scanderbeg
himself.''

Sir Francis doubted not but there would come
abroad a narrative of his life, and therefore added no
more, only to tell his correspondent that he had this

---

[1] C. P. xxxix. 142.

relation from the gentleman's own mouth that the Duke employed. He saw the commission all written by the Duke's own hand, but he would not let him see the private instructions he had, but assured him that all the army of Ireland could not have done it, nor was any other way left but that which the Duke took.

There was subsequently published an account of Redmond O'Hanlon's death, in the form of a letter from a gentleman in Dublin to a person of quality, his friend, in the country. It gives the copy of a warrant from the Duke of Ormonde to Mr. William Lucas of Drumintyne, dated the 4th of March, 1681, to compass the taking or death of Redmond O'Hanlon,—and Mr. Lucas's warrant to Art (or Arthur) O'Hanlon to take or kill Redmond, dated the 4th of April, 1681. From the time of issuing the Proclamation with the reward of £200 for Redmond's head, Redmond was accompanied by Arthur O'Hanlon and O'Shiel, who acted as guards or sentinels.

On the day of Redmond's death it was O'Shiel's turn to be *vedette*, or *Centinel perdu* (as it is called in the account of Redmond's life), and Arthur sate by him in an empty cabin while he took some sleep. They had met Redmond by appointment to watch some traders coming from the fair of Banbridge (Eight Mile Bridge, as it was then called).

As Redmond lay sound asleep at two o'clock in the afternoon, Arthur poured the contents of his blunder-buss into Redmond's breast, and immediately ran off for aid. In the meantime O'Shiel coming into the cabin, and Redmond being still alive, requested him to cut off his head as soon as his fast-ebbing life should be over, to keep it from being the spoil and triumph of his enemies.

This O'Shiel did, and ran away with it. The trunk was then brought into Newry, and messengers sent out to search for the head.

Among the payments by order of the Lord Lieutenant and Council, there appears One Hundred Pounds paid to Arthur O'Hanlon, 6th of May, 1681, for killing the torie Redmond O'Hanlon; and on 12th December in the same year, to John Mullin, as reward for killing Loughlin O'Hanlon, Fifty Pounds. Two Pamphlets concerning this event were purchased by Rooney of Anglesea Street, bookseller, at the sale of the Marquis of Hastings's Library, at Donnington Park, Nottinghamshire, in January, 1869.—One is entitled "Redmond O'Hanlon, Count Hanlon's Downfall, or a true and exact account of the Killing that Arch-traytor and Tory, Redmond O'Hanlon, by Art O'Hanlon, one of his own party, on the 25th of April, 1681, near Eight-Mile Bridge, in the county of Down, being the copy of a Letter written by a Country Gentleman (now in Dublin), to a person of Quality (his friend) in the country. Dublin: Printed for William Winter, Bookseller, at the Wandering Jew in Castle Street. 1681."

The other: " Redmond O'Hanlon,—the Life and Death of the incomparable and indefatigable Tory, Redmond O'Hanlon, commonly called Count Hanlon, in a Letter to Mr. R. A., in Dublin (dated 1st August, 1681). Printed for John Foster, at the King's Arms, Skinner Row. 1682."—The late Marquis of Hastings, descended from Sir George Rawdon, of Moira, in the county of Antrim; and from him probably the two pamphlets came.

On the 21st of September, 1863, leaving Rostrevor

for Newry at an early hour, I went from thence alone on foot to spend a day in the Fews mountains.

My principal object was to visit one of these primeval subterranean stone chambers, like the celebrated cave at Grange, near Drogheda, described in Lewis's Topographical Dictionary as lying in the townland of Augh-na-cloch-Mullan (meaning, as I afterwards found, the field of the stone or tomb of Mullan), in the parish of Killevy; and I purposed to return thence to Rostrevor by the ferry at Narrow Water, so as to pass on my journey the ancient ruins of Killevy Church, lying at the foot of Slieve Gullion, on the eastern side—a strangely large church and ancient graveyard for so wild and mountainous a district. When I got near Augh-na-cloch-Mullan, I was still asking the way, but found the place little known. At length I came to a house, and, knocking at the door, a hearty old woman came out to me, and went for her as hearty old husband, who was somewhat lame, I perceived, as he clambered out of the potato garden, where he had been digging some for supper. He guessed the place I wanted to see, though he did not know it by its Irish name ; and no wonder ; for I said it broad, as near as I could to the way it is written, while it ought to be sounded like Anna-gle-million. " Oh! you want Redmond O'Hanlon's Cave," and he pointed to a field about half a mile off, and in the middle of it some old blackthorns, near some huge mossy granite stones— thorns that so often mark in Ireland ancient sites ; the reason being, that they protect the remains ; for no one would dare to stir old solitary bushes : they are the haunts of " good people." He seemed surprised at the interest I took in it, and doubted the answers I gave him. But when I pulled out a wax candle and matches I had brought to light up the cave, he said, with emphasis, " By dad, but I would like to go with you : you are after some of Redmond O'Hanlon's goold. Will you promise me a share of what you find?" I promised to call in on him on my way back, and walked off to Anna-gle-million. But I found, to my regret, that the huge upright stones that had formed the cave underground to the centre of what had once been a barrow or earth mound, had been first made a quarry of by the masons when Mr. Synnot's new house at Ballymoyer was built, some thirty years ago ; and since then this curious monument of the earliest times has been utterly ruined and nearly effaced. I returned a wiser man. My hosts had got brown bread and sweet milk ready for me. They had a mountain freshness of face and heart, and seemed to live for each other. Like Philemon and Baucis—

> " Hymenée et l'amour par des desirs constants
> Avoient uni leurs cœurs dès leur plus doux printemps.
> Ils surent cultiver sans se voir assistés,
> Leur enclos et leur champ par deux fois vingt étés :
> Eux seuls ils composoient toute leur république
> Heureux de ne devoir à pas un domestique
> Le plaisir ou le gré des soins qu'ils se rendoient."

Redmond, though a felon to the English, was a hero to the Irish. One cannot but think of the anecdote mentioned by the late Earl of Carnarvon, concerning the tories of Greece, showing similar sentiments arising from not very dissimilar circumstances. In his reminiscences of Athens and the Morea he tells of a

conversation he had with a shepherd in the woods of
Sparta, during his travels there in 1839. He and his
travelling companion were near a monument erected
to the memory of Leonidas. "And who," they asked
this shepherd, "was Leonidas," in order to test his
knowledge of the history of his country ? " I cannot
tell you precisely," he answered, " but certainly a very
famous man, was he not ?" " He was indeed," replied
Lord Carnarvon. " A *Capitani* surely," rejoined the
shepherd. "Something higher still," we said. " Ah,"
he replied, brightening up, with a peculiar smile of
intelligence, as if he had just divined our meaning, and
as if a chord had been struck to which his mind fami-
liarly responded, " He was a πρῶτος κλεφτ," a Grand or
Leading tory.[1]

For in such a country to be a law-abiding people
was thought to be mean-spirited, and to be another
name for submission to tyrants. Thus, too, the name
of Redmond O'Hanlon is kept fresh in the memory of
the Irish of Ulster.

In the neighbourhood of his former haunts every
cave is " Redmond O'Hanlon's parlour," " Redmond
O'Hanlon's stable," or " Redmond O'Hanlon's bed."
And in a small ancient grave-yard near Tanderagee,
the former seat of the O'Hanlons, any Irish peasant
will point out among the green mounds, the greenest
of all, Redmond O'Hanlon's grave:

[1] Reminiscences of Athens and the Morea : Extracts from a Journal in
1839, by the late Earl of Carnarvon. Edited by his Son, the present Earl.
John Murray, London. 1869.

# PART THIRD.

## CHAPTER I.

### THE HISTORY OF THE THREE BRENNANS, TORIES OF THE COUNTY OF KILKENNY.

IN the month of November, 1683, all Ireland rang with the news of the capture, at Chester, of three proclaimed "Tories and Rebells" of the county of Kilkenny and adjacent districts, named Brennan. They were safe in Chester jail. The Mayor of Chester announced the good news to the Duke of Ormonde, then Lord Lieutenant of Ireland, at his house in St. James's Square, London. The Chief Justice of Ireland congratulated the Duke. The Duke thanked the Mayor of Chester, and requested him to have a careful eye on the prisoners.

During the three years before their arrest they had robbed His Majesty's good subjects of £12,000 and upwards, in cash. They had been tried, convicted, and sentenced, and brought out to be hanged ; but had been rescued from the very scaffold and the hands of the hangman. They were " proclaimed" as tories and rebels in Ireland ; they were pursued by armed men ; rewards were offered for their heads—but in vain. After lying quietly for some time at Ringsend, then the port of Dublin, they sailed thence to North Wales—their horses (described as delicate ones, or as we should now say, well-bred), with one of their comrades as groom, in one vessel, themselves in another.

They were "rich in apparel,"—wore swords which they attempted to draw on their captors in the streets of Chester. They were heavily shackled in jail ; yet before long all Ireland rang again (as did now London itself) with their escape. For, after a few days they had overpowered the jailer and his warders, and opened the prison doors for themselves.

All this is strange ; but stranger still is it, that they are next year back in Ireland, and, with a band of tories, break into Kilkenny Castle, the Duke of Ormonde's chief residence in Ireland, and carry off the Duke's plate. But strangest of all, they are "taken into protection" a few months afterwards by the Lord Lieutenant of Ireland, and allowed the use of their horses and travelling arms, in order to the discovering their accomplices, and "doing service," as it was called, that is, killing other tories; and the Grand Jury of the county of Kilkenny actually "present" it as their advice that they should be taken into permanent protection, as the best course to suppress robberies and felonies in that part of the kingdom.

The O'Brennans or Brennans were an ancient tribe or Sept of Ossory ; and "The Brennan's country" was the northern part of the county of Kilkenny, where it thrusts itself in a kind of tongue between the Queen's county and the county of Carlow. Its capital is the town of Castlecomer. The district was called Odogh, Idough, or Edough, and anciently extended beyond the bounds of the barony of Fassach-Dinin, its present limits, eastward into Carlow and westward into Queen's county. The Brennans however, retiring gradually

before the advancing early English planters (the
feudal tenants of William Earl Marshal), from the
lower and more fertile portions of the ancient territory
of Odogh, in "the fair wide plain of the Nore," betook
themselves to the hills round Castlecomer.

At Castlecomer, at the junction of the Dinin and
another stream, stood and still stands one of those pre-
historic green mounds used by the ancient Irish at the
election of their chiefs.   Here he stood when elected,
shown by the Brehon to the whole tribe, and, below
him, with his foot on the mound, the Tanist or next
successor.

From the summit, in view of all the tribe, the new
elected Chief distributed wands to the subordinate
Chiefs, emblems of their authority.   Comer or Comber is the name in Irish for the junction of two streams,
and at such places mounds are frequent, as so well
suited for the purpose of these elections.

The O'Brennans were in early times a tribe of
dignity, as is inferred from the intermarriage of
Donough Mac Giolla Phadraig, who died in A.D. 1039,
head of the tribes of Upper Ossory, with a daughter of
the O'Brennans.   These Mac Giolla Phadraigs, Nor-
manized their name into Fitzpatrick, and became, in
Henry the Eighth's time, so friendly with the English,
that one of them was ennobled by the Barony, and
subsequently, the Earldom of Upper Ossory.[1]

The O'Brennans maintained themselves in considerable independence in Fassa-Dinin until the reign of
Charles the First.

[1] For the early history see a paper by the Rev. James Graves.—Proceedings of the Kilkenny Archæological Society. Vol. 1.   Also Life of
Wandesford, by Thomas Comber, LL.D. 12mo. Cambridge. 1770.

In the eighth year of that King's reign (*i.e.*, in the year 1633), Thomas Lord Wentworth, afterwards created Earl of Strafford, came over as Lord Deputy of Ireland, bringing in his train Christopher Wandesford, Esq., whom he made Master of the Rolls in Ireland, not then a judicial office, and soon afterwards knighted him. Sir Christopher Wandesford, in the year 1635, purchased from the Earl of Kildare the lands of Sigginstown, or Jigginstown, contiguous to the town of Naas. But the Lord Deputy, taking a liking to it, Wandesford resigned it to him, and on it Strafford built (of red Dutch brick) " the battered old house of Jigginstown," often pointed at to this day as a monument of his disappointed ambition, for before it was finished Strafford's head was taken off, and it remained a ruin ever after. But Strafford declared it was intended for a Royal residence in a fine hunting district, and, if the King did not like it, it should be at his (Strafford's) own cost. He would pay, he said, for his own folly. Sir Christopher Wandesford had therefore to look out for another purchase. That which he fixed his eye upon was the territory of Idough, or Edough,[1] in the county of Kilkenny, " found by Inquisition taken at Kilkenny on the 11th May, 1635, to be in the Crown," and that the tribe or Sept of the O'Brennans were " mere Irish," and had no title but held it " by strong hand" (a title they had probably held it by from before the Birth of Christ). The

---

[1] It is best to write " Edough," as the name is pronounced. The English are the only people in Europe that make the I long. Iveagh (the M'Genis territory), was always pronounced " Evagh," as appears from contemporary documents.

I

Earl of Ormonde, however, and Sir Robert Ridgway, Earl of Londonderry, claimed some title derived through a grant of King James the First. And there was an older English title still, derived from Strongbow's intermarriage with Eva MacMurrough. This marriage brought all Leinster to Strongbow, and Strongbow having no heir male, it passed to his daughter and only child, married to William Earl Marshal, and he having only five daughters and heirs, it gavelled into five parts. The Duke of Norfolk, in 1639 (descended from one daughter), claimed the county of Kilkenny as his inheritance. "Has he not," wrote Strafford, "got Edough off his stomach yet ?"

Sir Christopher Wandesford, having purchased the Earl of Ormonde's and Sir Robert Ridgway's rights for £2,000 (Dr. Comber says £20,000), the territory of Edough was conveyed to Sir Christopher on 25th July, 1637. The Brennans, during all this negociation for the purchase, looked upon themselves as the true owners, and engaged the Lords Mountgarret and Maltravers to be their Solicitors at the Court in England, and declined to enter into any surrender of their rights, notwithstanding the various solicitations of Sir Christopher to them for that purpose. This stubbornness on their part, and gentleness on Wandesford's part, suited not the overbearing spirit of the Lord Deputy. "He would have no man to question his orders," he said, "and would make an Act of State in Ireland to be as powerful as an Act of Parliament." He had come over to turn Ireland into a Royal fortress or place of arms, where, unimpeded by any Parliament, the King should have money and men at his absolute command, so as to be able thence to subdue his

rebellious Kingdoms of England and Scotland. And
we learn from the impeachment of this despotic servant
of the Crown by the Commons of England (April,
1640,) the measures he took to break and subdue the
Brennans to his friend Wandesford's will. In 1638,
the year after the purchase of Edough, one Richard
Butler, it seems, was still in possession of the Castle
of Castlecomer, and offered, as well as the Brennans,
some opposition to Sir Christopher's agents. The Earl
of Strafford thereupon sent down a sufficient body of
soldiers, who seized the fathers and mothers of about
one hundred families and brought them up to Dublin
to be imprisoned in the Castle of Dublin and other
jails.[1]

After such tyranny and violence, used in Sir Christopher Wandesford's behalf by his patrons, it would
not have been surprising if some bloody retribution had
been exacted by the Brennans. But no worse crime
was alleged against any of them than the taking of
some of Sir Christopher's sheep, and this probably proceeded rather out of their claim to the land the sheep
fed on, than robbery. On one occasion when Wandesford's seneschal and other officers proceeded to search
for the missing sheep, they were plentifully entertained
by one of the chief men of the Sept with excellent

---

[1] The 15th Article of the Impeachment is as follows :—" And in the said
12th year of His Majesty's reign (A.D. 1638), the said Earl of Strafford did
traitorously send certain troops of horse and foot to expel Richard Butler
from the possession of Castlecomber, in the territory of Idough, and, in
like manner, expelled divers of His Majesty's subjects from their houses,
families and possessions, as—namely, Edward Brennan, Owen O'Brennan,
and divers others, to the number of about one hundred families, and carried
them and their wives prisoners to Dublin, and there detained them until they
yielded up their respective estates and rights."—C.P. xlix., 296,

mutton dressed in various shapes, while their host took care to let them know where it came from by throwing the head and skin with Sir Christopher's brand on it over the shoulders of his shepherd as he, in the seneschal's company, was leaving the bawn.

O'Brennan being subsequently condemned to death for the robbery, Sir Christopher obtained his pardon, moved, perhaps, by the above-board dealing of the man. Sir Christopher died not long after the purchase of Edough, and there is reason to think that it had no inconsiderable share in bringing him to the grave. He became possessed of it in 1637. The year 1640 was the crisis of his patron Strafford's fate. Strafford had assembled an army of 8,000 men about Belfast and Carrickfergus for the invasion of Scotland by order of the King, who was to advance across the border from York to engage the Scottish rebels in front. Strafford was to land in Scotland and attack them on their flank and rere ; and, " having whipped them home in their own blood," as he said, the Royal Army of victorious English and Irish were then to march towards London to give the discontented English a lesson. But the whole scheme failed. The Scottish Army, knowing that they had friends even in the King's army, suddenly, on the 20th August, 1640, crossed the border, being the very day the King left London, and when the King reached York he found himself obliged by many, even of his own nobility, to enter into a treaty with the Scots, who had gained Newcastle, and to engage to call a Parliament to raise funds to pay the Scots the cost of their invasion. But the discontented both of England and Scotland had the further design of impeaching Laud and Strafford. And no sooner did Lord

Strafford arrive in London to attend the opening of this
" Parliament of Parliaments," in November, 1640, than
Pym and his friends' impeached him, and on the 12th
of May following the head of this tyrannical Lord
Lieutenant of Ireland fell at the block on Tower Hill.
Sir Christopher Wandesford was his deputy.  In April,
1640, Strafford had been called over from Ireland by
the King to aid him by his counsel ; but he was
arrested, and he continued a prisoner in the Tower for
the short remainder of his life.  During this period
Sir Christopher Wandesford supplied Strafford's place
in Ireland.  But Wandesford, having knowledge of
the heavy charges of tyranny preparing against his
now imprisoned friend, the Lord Lieutenant of Ireland,
and amongst the rest his violent proceedings in the
matter of the purchase of Edough, sank brokenhearted
to the grave from a foresight of the ruin to come.  He
died on the 3rd of December, 1640, and his biographer
remarks that the Irish, at the Lord Deputy's interment,
raised their peculiar lamentations, a signal honour paid
to him by that people, probably the last time the Irish
cry was heard at a funeral in Dublin.  His fears,
perhaps, had the effect of awakening his conscience,
for by his Will, made on the 2nd of October, 1640,
only a few weeks before his death, he endeavoured to
offer the former native proprietors of Edough some
compensation for their lost lands.  This he effected by
executing a trust deed on the 2nd of September, 1640,
whereby he conveyed the territory of Edough to John
Bramhall (Bishop of Derry), Sir Edward Osborne,
Major Norton, and William Wandesford, for the term
of 41 years to answer the trusts of his will ; and on

the 2nd of October following he made his Will, containing this provision :—

"Whereas, also, the natives of Idough, called Brennans, who have for many years possessed the same, have several times refused such proffers of benefit as I thought good out of my own private charity and conscience to tender unto them—not that I ever believed, either by Law or Equity, I could be compelled to give them any consideration at all for their pretended interest—my will is that the trustees aforesaid shall, out of the said rents, pay unto so many of them (the said Brennans) or their children, as by a Commission out of Chancery shall be found to have been the reputed possessors and terr-tenants of the lands at the time of the finding of the Office of Idough for His Majesty, dated 21st May, 1635, so much money severally as a lease for 21 years of the moiety of those lands so in their possession respectively, shall be by the said Commissioners valued to have been worth unto the said possessors at the time of finding the said Office after the common course of bargaining."

The breaking out of the Irish Rebellion on 23rd October, 1641, would, of course, have hindered the Brennans from obtaining the benefit of Sir Christopher's legacy, if they had been disposed to claim it, or had they known of it. The whole Kingdom was thenceforward for many years a scene of ruin and confusion. The Castle of Castlecomer was regularly besieged in the month of December, 1641, by a portion of Lord Mountgarret's army of Irish, containing, it may well be supposed, a large contingent of Brennans.

After holding out for eighteen weeks under Captain Farrer, the garrison surrendered the Castle to the as-

sailants, who consisted of about three companies under
the command, amongst others, of Captain Edward
Brennan. By the terms of the surrender, the garrison
were to be escorted safely by a body of Irish, under
the command of Captain Dempsey, towards the English garrison of Ballylinan in the Queen's County,
about fifteen miles distant to the Northward—oaths
being mutually passed by the officers of each party to
protect the other from the violence of their countrymen respectively. Captain Dempsey and the Irish
duly performed their engagement, and brought the
Castlecomer garrison to a place where they were met
by Captain Grimes, or Graham, the Commander of
Ballylinan, with his forces, and, having delivered them
safely, were on their way back to Castlecomer, when
they were treacherously attacked and put to flight by
Captain Grimes, assisted by some of the Castlecomer
refugees. Sir Christopher Wandesford had left his
cousin, William Wandesford, in charge of his estate at
Castlecomer ; but he and Lady Wandesford escaped
before the siege—he (according to Lady W.'s account)
" in an Irish disguise," with Sir Christopher's principal
writings, " secure in his trousers." When the forces
of the Parliament, in 1650, had recovered the county
of Kilkenny, they must have sequestrated the Wandesford estate as a Royalist or Protestant delinquent's ;
for his heir was obliged to sue for it in Cromwell's
Court of Claims, and there obtained a Decree of " Constant Good Affection," and was restored to all the
property which Lord Deputy Wandesford died possessed
of. This district, therefore, underwent less change
than other parts of the country where the ancient proprietors and their families were driven out by Crom-

·wellian planters ; and it may be from this circumstance
that there is less recounted of the Brennans among
the many bands of tories in this neighbourhood in
the early years following the Restoration than of other
names.

Sir Christopher Wandesford, Lord Deputy, was succeeded on his death, in December, 1640, by his son,
Sir Christopher Wandesford, Bart.  In 1679 two-and-
twenty of the Brennans filed their Bill in Chancery
against him, claiming the legacies left them by the
Deputy's Will, and on the 10th of June, 1686, obtained
a Decree of the Chancellor in their favour on making
out what their ancestors were possessed of, and their
several titles and demands, and it was referred to one
of the Four Masters in Chancery to examine and settle
them ; but owing to the death of Sir Christopher
Wandesford, on the 26th of February, 1687, and the
Civil War or Revolution that commenced in the following year and ended with the victory of William
of Orange at the Battle of the Boyne, no further
proceedings were had in the suit.

Soon after the accession of King William and Queen
Mary, Sir Christopher Wandesford, son of the late Sir
Christopher, and grandson of Deputy Wandesford, took
measures to clear his estate of the claims of the Brennans.
In 1694 he presented his petition to the King and Queen,
and prayed that the forfeited rights of the Brennans,
under the decree in Chancery, should be granted to
him for his services and sufferings.  His grandfather,
he said, on the 2nd of October, being then Lord
Deputy, made his will, leaving legacies to several
native Irish, then tenants of some of his lands of
Idough, being part of the Sept called the Brennans.

In the Rebellion of 1641 the Brennans, he said, possessed themselves of all his estate and the stock upon it, and burnt and destroyed all his buildings and improvements to the value of many thousands of pounds, and murthered many of his English tenants, and enjoyed his estate for ten years after without making any satisfaction.

The Sept of the Brennans (he continued) being still very numerous, were a great terror to the English inhabitants of that country, and frequently committed many great robberies and murthers, and were in arms for the late King James.

And the Petitioner (Sir Christopher) being in arms very early for the service of His Majesty, then Prince of Orange, the Brennans procured the Lord Tyrconnell (the celebrated Dick Talbot) to seize upon his estate, as forfeited on that account, and got into possession of it, and enjoyed it for a considerable time without rendering any account of the profits.

He was soon after, he said, at the cost of making outlaws of the Brennans, who had been adversaries of his father, and had obtained the Decree. This was with the aim of having their claims for the legacies, under his grandfather's Will, vested in the Crown as forfeited. The whole being only preliminary to obtaining a grant of the benefit of the Decree, and thus extinguishing for ever the claims of the Brennans, and clearing his estate of Idough of this cloud upon the title.

And all this he successfully accomplished.[1]

---

[1] These proceedings are calendared in Treasury Papers 1694, Vol. 30, No. 1, Public Record Office, London. The names of the Brennans, who obtained the Decree and were outlawed, are given by Sir Richard Levinge,

Sir Christopher Wandesford was well warranted in charging some of the Brennans with great robberies, when it appears, as by the opening statement, that the three Brennans had, in three years, robbed His Majesty's good subjects of not £12,000, as there mentioned, but £18,000 in cash. At this time, in the year 1683, the race of proprietors, despoiled by the Cromwellians, had, most of them, sunk into the grave, and the tories were degenerating into common robbers. The first notice of these three Brennans is in a letter of Otway, Bishop of Ossory, in the beginning of the year 1683, to the Earl of Arran, Lord Deputy for Ormonde. They had already become notorious ; for the Bishop described them as those very Brennans who had done, and were still doing, so much mischief in that country, and had, the morning before, by a wile, lured one of the witnesses against them into a wood, and there, with horrid cruelty, cut out his tongue.[1] The Bishop enlarges upon the barbarity of the deed. But, of course, makes no mention of his

the Attorney-General, in his report to the Lords Justices, dated 13th Oct. 1694, as follows :—

John Brennan, late of Levin, gentleman ; John Brennan, late of Crott, gentleman ; Owen Brennan, late of Kildonoghinkelly, gentleman ; Farr Brennan, late of Crotten logh, gentleman ; Patrick Brennan, late of Cloneen, gentleman ; Loghlin Brennan, late of the same, gentleman ; Loghlin Brennan, son of James, late of the same, gentleman ; Margaret Brennan, late of Kildonoghinkelly ; Mortagh Brennan, late of Kilrobbing, gentleman ; Anastas Brennan, late of the same ; Donagh Brennan, late of Rathcally, gentleman ; Elinor Brennan, late of Dungillinagh, spinster ; William Brennan Fitz-John, late of Smithstown, gentleman ; James Brennan, of the same, gentleman ; Margaret Brennan, late of Turlave, spinster ; Edward Brennan, late of Ballyhoman, gentleman ; Donagh Brennan, late of Kilkenny, gentleman ; Edmond Brennan, late of Cruttin, gentleman ; and by the outlawry and attainder, the rights of which they, or any of them, had against Sir Christopher, the Petitioner's father, by the Decree in ¡Chancery, are forfeited to the Crown and in their Majesties' disposal.

[1] Otway, Bishop of Ossory to Arran, Feb. 5, 1688. C. P. ccxvi., 129.

own conduct so reprehended by the Earl of Ossory in cutting off the head of a proclaimed tory in his own court-yard at Killalla ; for he had been bishop of Kil, lalla before his translation to the Diocese of Ossory.

In the following June as Alexander Marshal of Lis- burn, in the county of Antrim and two other merchants were riding from Ballynakill to Kilcullen, they were overtaken on Ballyraggett Heath, in the county of Kilkenny, by the three Brennans, well mounted, armed with swords, carbines, and pistols. They knocked them off their horses, dragged them into an old fort, and there robbed them of goods and money to the value of £100.[1]  They next robbed the house of Mr. Bolton, grandson of Lord Chancellor Bolton, at Bra- zeel, seven miles north of Dublin, which for the sum taken (wrote Chief Justice Keatinge) and the faint prosecution of the thieves, exceeded all the rob- beries the Chief Justice had ever heard of. Mr. Bolton would incur no expense in prosecuting them. These Brennans (adds the Chief Justice), were per- sons convict, who after sentence and after being brought to the gallows to be executed made their escape in a way too tedious to tell in that letter. Chief Justice Keatinge being concerned for the justice of the kingdom issued his warrants into the adjacent counties, particularly the Queen's County, where the Brennans had many friends and relations, and got his cousin, Jack Warren, to hunt them so close that they were obliged to fly,—and yet while flying they still robbed. But the Chief Justice having heard that they had reached the King's Head at Ringsend, then a place of departure for vessels from Dublin, he had the house,

[1] Sworn information of Alex. Marshal, 19th October, 1683. C. P. xl., 85.

which was kept by a Brennan, continually watched by his spies, but to no purpose. For no sooner was he gone to his country-seat at Lissen Hall,[1] than the three Brennans, with a boy of theirs, a cousin who had been boarded at that Inn, shipped themselves on board the Doggar boat whilst she was under sail, leaving their horses to be brought after them by their boy, and £53 in cobbs to be sent to them by bill on London by their landlord, who pretended to know nothing of them. Being recognized in Chester by Mr. Marshal as those that had robbed him on Ballyragget Heath, they were arrested for the robbery and committed to jail. They were extravagantly rich, the Chief Justice Keatinge heard, and would think nothing of giving £3,000 for a pardon or liberty to transport themselves to foreign parts.

He had heard they had made Sir Robert Reading their friend, but the Chief Justice scorned the tale.[2]

. Yet strange as it may seem they certainly had secured his favour. For, Sir Robert, writing to Arran on hearing of their capture, said he scarce knew how they could escape hanging, but hoped that His Excellency would remember the poor devils, and let them quit the Kingdom if they had had no hand in blood. And he believed his word would have some weight, as he it was that got them to quit Ireland when Captain Bishop and all the country could not catch them.[3]

Ormonde, in apprising Arran of their arrest at Chester, said they wore swords which they drew on

---

[1] In the parish of Swords, and county of Dublin.

[2] Chief Justice John Keatinge to James Clarke, Ormonde's servant in London, November 1st, 1683. C. P. xl., 100.

[3] Sir Robert Reading to the Earl of Arran, Lord Deputy. From London, 21st October, 1683. C. P. ccxvi.

their captors, and were "in greater splendour and plenty than belonged to any of their race."[1]

The Brennans were only two days in Chester jail, when they overpowered the jailer, took from him the prison keys, and set themselves free.

From the sworn information of Richard Wright, the keeper of the jail at the North gate of Chester, it appears that on the 19th of October, 1683, he received into his custody James O'Brennan, Patrick O'Brennan, and James O'Brennan called Tall James, charged with the highway robbery of Mr. Marshal on Ballyragget Heath in Ireland.

He was so careful of them that he kept them in irons, he said, all day, and when they were in bed took away their clothes. While he and his wife sat at supper (he deposed) in the lower room, called the hall, with the three Brennans well ironed,—and Thomas Greene, a prisoner for debt, employed by the jailer as his assistant, Tall James (he swore) spoke something in Irish to the other two; Little James, who sat beside the jailer, drew a knife and struck at his (Richard Wright's), throat, and wounded him in the arm which he had raised to protect his throat. Seizing the jailer he thrust his head under the bed, and stamped upon him with his knees, till, in fear of his life, he promised to be quiet. Tall James caught hold of Thomas Greene, and threatened to cut his throat, and getting him down, put him in irons. Patrick secured and terrified Mrs. Wright, the jailer's wife.

Patrick O'Brennan then went upstairs to the jailer's closet and brought down a sword and tuck, and with the keys he found there unlocked their fetters,—and

[1] Ormonde to Arran, London, 27th October, 1683. C. P. ccxix., 340.

taking the keys of the outer gate out of the jailer's pocket, let himself and his two fellow-prisoners free.

The jailer then went up to one of the upper windows to raise the alarm, but the prisoners ran back to the gate, and threatened to come in and kill him, only he bolted the gate on the inner side against them.

The only other person in Mr. Wright's service was a maid-servant, Mary Swettenham, and there is something characteristic of the Irishmen's treatment of this girl. According to her account she saw one of the Brennans on her mistress and she on the ground. She tried to pull him off, but failing, fled to the cellar and locked herself in. The Brennans came and promised to do her no hurt, and spoke her very fair, upon which she came out. One of them said to her, " Sweetheart, you and I, it may be, may meet again." " In another country then," said she. They bade her blow out the candle she had in her hand ; but she did not, but set it down, and they blew it out,—opened the prison doors, and went their way, and locked them after them.

The Earl of Arran, Lord Deputy, had suspicions of the good faith of the jailer. The Brennans could well pay him for conniving at their escape, as in two and a half years' time, according to Arran's account, they had robbed to the extent of £18,000. And there is something rank in the evidence he gives of his fear of them, locking his prisoners out and himself in, so that the door had to be cloven to let the Magistrates in, the Brennans having taken away the keys.[1]

---

[1] All the papers and proceedings with these details are to be found in C. P. Vol. xl.

The hue and cry was raised, and every effort made to capture the prisoners, but in vain. And the next that is heard of them is that they were back again in Ireland, and on the 17th of September, 1685, had broken into Kilkenny Castle, and out of the Duke's closet had carried off a pair of silver Andirons, a large silver Tankard, and the Ears of a silver Fountain (probably some ornamental plate for the dinner service), but the belly being too big to get out at the window it was left behind. They also carried off a box of plate, belonging to Captain Geo. Mathew, the Duke's half brother and land agent.[1] And now took place an occurrence that marks the defective organization of government of Ireland for the repression and discovery of crime. Could it be believed without evidence of the Carte Papers, that these Brennans, proclaimed tories, robbers, and outlaws,—who had robbed before this their latest robbery in Kilkenny Castle, to the extent of £18,000,—who had escaped from the very gallows in Ireland, and broke their prison in Chester—that these men should be taken into protection and employed to discover the lost plate ! At the instance of Captain George Mathew, the Earl of Clarendon, who had succeeded the Duke of Ormonde as Lord Lieutenant, took James Brennan of Crottenclough and Patrick Brennan of Killeshin into protection for seven months, on condition of discovering the lost plate, much to the disgust of Aungier, Earl of Longford, and others in Dublin, who regretted that Captain Mathew could find no better instruments. They were to be free of arrest and have

[1] Gerard Borr (Arran's Secretary), to the Earl of Arran, Dublin, 20th September, 1685. C. P. ccxvii., 124.

the use of their horses and firearms for travelling. Besides discovering the stolen silver plate, they were to make other tories and robbers amenable to justice. This protection is dated February 19th, 1683. And at the Assizes for the county of Kilkenny in March, 1687, the Grand Jury made their Presentment that they conceived there could be no better way to suppress robberies and felonies in those parts than to take these two Brennans into protection for a term of years.[1]

At this time Dick Talbot (made Duke of Tyrconnell), was Lord Lieutenant of Ireland for King James the Second., and one of the charges against him in the reign of the succeeding dynasty was that he had employed tories like the Brennans in his army. And it has been suggested that if the Irish army list of King James II. were searched, the names of the Brennans would probably appear amongst his officers or soldiers.

[1] See a paper on the Earlier History of the Brennans of Odough or Idough, by the Rev. James Graves, in the first Volume of the Proceedings of the Kilkenny Archæological Society.

HISTORY helps us no farther towards the fate and end
of the three Brennans. But the name and fame of
the tribe of Brennans survive in the work of Dr John
Brenan, author of the " Milesian Magazine," which
began its career of political, professional, and personal
satire in 1812, and lasted till 1825, during which Dr.
Brenan exhibited all the verve and inexhaustible wit
and humour of Rabelais.

Dr. John Brenan, M.D., was a man known to his
contemporaries as " The Turpentine Doctor," or " The
Wrestling Doctor,"—the first name for introducing
turpentine as a cure for child-bed fever, and " The
Wrestling Doctor " for his patronage of that sport.
By himself he was styled " Prince of Edough and
King of all the Wrestlers of all Ireland." In his
character of " Prince " he addressed the Duchess of
Richmond, wife of the Lord Lieutenant of Ireland
from 1807 to 1813, as an equal, having, he asserted,
as long and honourable an ancestry as the first man
then in Ireland, if there never was a Lord Lieutenant
in Dublin.

The Earl of Strafford (he informs the Duchess) gave
the Brennan Estate to Sir Christopher Wandesford,
his Secretary, and Wandesford, frightened at the fate
of Strafford, left £10,000 by his last Will to the
Brennans, and committed suicide (which only rests on
the wrestling doctor's authority, and is contrary to
fact). The Parliament (according to his account, and

K

his alone), ratified the legacy (which was perfectly good without ratification), and the legacy not having been paid, the accumulations were worth more, he said, than the Wandesford Estate. The true history of Strafford's tyranny towards the Brennans has been already set forth in the preceding pages.

Childbed fever was, in 1815, a nearly fatal disease and epidemic in the Rotundo Hospital. Dr. Brenan got himself admitted as a student (though a fully qualified physician) to the Lying-in Hospital, and unknown to the doctors of the establishment, effected some wonderful cures. But he was no sooner detected than he was turned out. For, as he makes Judge Bladderchops (his designation of Lord Norbury, from his constant puffing,) say, in one of his numerous and humorous trials—in this case it was "The Lying-in Hospital against Dr. Brenan," in Dec., 1815—addressing Dr. Brenan, in his sentence: "As well might my horse, Crop, sit here to try causes as you attempt what you have done on Dr. Hopkins' premises. The patients are his property—his game—that you have poached upon. You have no more right to cure in his demesne than you had to kill partridges on my estate in Tipperary. You ought to know that the women in childbed in the hospital were the subjects of Dr. Hopkins—a man appointed by the State ; a loyal Protestant, that signed the petition against Popery. Dr. Hopkins was, in some respects, the Lord's anointed, as deriving under his present Majesty, who, I am glad to hear (this was during King George the Third's confinement as a lunatic), is able to ride about Windsor Park and drink a pint of hock. Curing Dr. Hopkins' dying women, let me tell you, is contrary (I won't say to Dr. Hopkins'

Crown), but contrary to his peace and dignity before the nurses and pupils, and the porter and housekeeper, and renders your sentence such as will allowe me to give you no hope of mitigation ; and the sentence of the Court is this:—That you, Dr. Brenan, be brought to the place from whence you came to the house of Dr. Jack Famish,[1] and there be boarded for three meals a-day until you be dead, dead, dead ! and the fasting, I hope, will be good for your soul ; and the Lord have mercy on your small guts.—God save the King ! " Jack Famish (he says elsewhere) kept his whole family on a potted herring and a naggin of turpentine on last Christmas Day ; better, Jack declared, than on a leg of mutton and two bunches of turnips.

Dr. Brenan was born in 1774, and, according to his own account, was left, with other orphan brothers and sisters, to the care of a mother who was bribed by an attorney, of the name of Robert Cornwall, to be allowed to make away (for his costs) with the paternal property, which consisted of part of the town of Carlow. The Castle Hill, and the ancient (once royal) Castle of Carlow itself—where for many ages was kept a Second Court of Exchequer in Ireland—formed part of their estate. Under the Castle is the Bridge over the Barrow. In two minutes one is in the Queen's County, near the cradle of the Brennans. The Castle Hill and the whole estate was an island, as it were, formed by the Barrow and the Barrin, let for buildings on leases to expire in four years. Cornwall was employed to get in a debt due to the estate, and ran up a Bill of Costs to £200, and brought the estate to

---

[1] Dr. Joseph Burke. He and his family deeply felt (and still feel) the imputation ; probably causeless.

a sale, and had it sold, says Dr. Brenan, to a nominee of his own for £300, being then (with the " Tobacco Meadows," consisting of nine plantation acres of building ground,) worth £10,000. All this is set forth in Dr. Brenan's letters to Lord Manners in the May number of " The Milesian Magazine " of the year 1812, Lord Manners being just then appointed Chancellor of Ireland.

The Magazine had only been established in the previous month. It commenced with an attack on Watty Cox of the " Union (or United Irish) Star," which had etchings of Yeomen flogging Irish peasants in '98, ravishing women, burning cabins, with Lieutenant Jack Hepenstal, of Yeomanry fame, who " was himself judge, jury, gallows and all." He was so tall and strong that, throwing the noose round the Croppy's neck and the rope over his shoulders, he hanged, or half hanged, his victim as he marched on. Dr. Brenan signalised " The Union Star " as the " Murder Gazette," for its marking out men for assassination. The frontispiece to the first or April number of " The Milesian Magazine," in 1812, is entitled *Sidus Coxicum* (or the Cox Constellation), and represents the head of Watty Cox in the sky, with the motto " *Occidit que legendo* " (the reading of it, causes murder). Showers of daggers are seen falling like meteors on the victims below on earth, amongst them Major Sirr, noted for arresting Lord Edward Fitzgerald (by Watty Cox's aid, as Brenan alleged), Dr. Troy (Roman Catholic Archbishop of Dublin), Arthur Guinness the brewer. " Freemasons (continues Dr. Brenan's explanation of the plate) bleed in every pore. Black masons are stabbed through the neck, Red through

the heart, and Blue through the lungs. Dr. Troy
stands upon the Cross and Missal, and meets Cox's
dagger officially, or as a Roman Catholic Bishop, for
the crime of going to the place where Watty Cox was
armourer, spy, and eavesdropper, viz., the Castle.
Robert Emmet receives a posthumous dagger on the
gallows, which alludes (according to Dr. Brenan) to
Watty's pamphlet (A.D. 1803) in defence of Watty's
old friend, Major Sirr, against Emerson's claim to the
reward for taking Captain Russell. . . . . Judge
Bladderchops, he continues, is hit *à cheval* (riding) ;
Sartgee, the Hottentot Venus, is there, and Dr.
Drumsnuffle, adds Dr. Brenan, to show that consummate beauty in one sex and consummate stupidity in
the other, are not exempt from the assaults of a man
bent on blood and politics like ' The Union Star' Man.

As Dr. Brenan's talent for satire developed itself,
he thought it necessary to take up some position of a
patriotic kind, and he chose that of an Anti-Veto Man
—that is to say, to oppose the Veto on the appointment of Irish Bishops, which the English Government
sought for by underhand arrangement with the Pope.

The politics of Ireland were, at that time, in the
hands of the Catholic Committee, consisting, as of old,
of certain of the ancient Catholic aristocracy of Ireland, of English race, as the Earl of Fingal, Viscount
Netterville, Major Bryan, Jenkinstown, in the County
of Kilkenny, commonly called (for his importance and
by way of caricature) King of the Romans, and some
barristers of talent and political capacity, as Daniel
O'Connell, Denys Scully (author of the work called
the Penal Laws affecting the Irish Catholics after the
concessions made in 1793), Mr Fin, a kinsman or con-

nexion of O'Connell's; and many others. The
Catholic Committee were in favour of the Veto, as
they hoped, if this concession was made, they should
get at once into Parliament, and a free career be opened
to their talents. Amongst the Veto Men were " Nine
consenting Prelates, Who'd make us spiritual helots.'
The Catholic Committee were engaged in selecting the
members of a deputation to send to London with their
petition for the removal of the Duke of Richmond,
when they were informed by a public letter of the
Chief Secretary to the Lord Lieutenant, Wellesley-
Pole (called always Poole), brother of Lord Wellington, afterwards the celebrated Waterloo Duke, that
they were contravening the provisions of the Convention Act—in other words, making the proposed Deputation representative.

In the first number of " The Milesian Magazine "
appeared " The Major's Petition ; a new play, performed at the Little Theatre, Capel-street, with un-
bounded applause."

" Barny, Barny, buck or doe ! " (begins Dr. Brenan's
lampoon).

> " Barny, Barny, buck or doe,
> Who shall with the petition go ?
> Who shall carry the rebuke
> Of the Papists 'gainst the Duke ?
> Who shall tell our gracious Prince
> That he makes religion wince ?
> That he keeps a knave and fool,
> And his name is Wellesley Pole,
> That writes saucy, scoundrel letters
> To the Papists for his betters ?
> That this country badly thrives
> While its Viceroy plays at Fives ;

And a grievance full as great is,
He drinks punch and eats potatoes?
Answer, quickly, as I call,
What say you, my Lord Fingal?

LORD FINGAL:

Once it stood a standing rule
To insult me as a fool.
Passiveness, I find, is bad;
Now, you use me like one mad.
What! Scout Viceroys for a Major,
Because Viceroys make a guager.[1]
Take the reason I won't go:
There's a corn upon my toe!

Barny, Barny, buck or doe,
Who shall with the petition go?
Come, Lord Southwell, what say you?

LORD SOUTHWELL:

One word is quite as good as two.
I see every disposition
Not to go with your petition.

Barny, Barny, buck or doe,
My Lord Netterville will go?

LORD NETTERVILLE:

I was very sick before;
Your petition makes me more.
Sick and sore, and much afraid
That a foolish game you played,
When you made out this petition,
Which I'll touch,—on no condition.

Barny, Barny, buck, or doe,
Who shall with the petition go?
Come, Lord Gormanston, and say
Will you with it post away?

[1] This alludes to the appointment of John Gifford, Esq., to a place in the Customs Department—a man who had supported Cruelty Camden, said Dr. Brenan, and "free quarters" and opposed "Croppy Corney," as Earl Cornwallis was called in 1798, like Clemency Canning, in the Indian Mutiny of 1857, for his humanity.

LORD GORMANSTON:

All petitions against Kings,
Or Vicegerents, are bad things.
Bankrupts such petitions bear
· Much more safely than a peer.
If there's none in your Committee,
They are plenty in the city.
Your petition, I won't bear it,
And I counsel you to tear it.

 Barny, Barny, buck or doe,
 Who shall with the petition go ?
 By your answer 'twill be seen.
 What say you, my Lord Killeen ?

LORD KILLEEN :

If my father goes, I'll go ;
But the corn that's on his toe
Makes me think there's little chance
That he'll lead the Major's dance.
But if he bears the petition,
I'm your post-boy with submission.

 Barny, Barny, buck or doe,
 Who shall with the petition go ?
 Will you go, my Lord Kenmare ?

LORD KENMARE :

For God's sake, my feelings spare !
The devouring Viceroy-Dukes
May suit statesmen who give pukes,
Gambling politicians, Majors ;
Briefless lawyers, fit for guagers ;
Upstarts—obscure jack-a-napes—
Who have bailiffs at their capes.
Such employments ill accord
With a gentleman or lord.
The task you offer I resent
As both mad and impudent.

 Barny, Barny, buck or doe,
 Who shall with the petition go ?
 We cannot, sure, be at a loss
 When we find out Castleross.

Say, great son of Lord Kenmare,
Will you the petition bear ?

LORD CASTLEROSS.

Never did I, since you knew me,
Feel such honour as you do me,
When you place me in this station ;
And, believe my declaration,
As I hope to meet salvation,
The cause of my renunciation
Is want of health and inclination.

LORD FFRENCH :

I declare, upon my conscience,
On the matter, I've but one sense,
Though there's things in the petition
Of which I would wish omission.
What I mean is the rebuke
Against Pole and 'gainst the Duke.
But if you bid me break their nose
My act should ne'er your will oppose ;
And, though by it my life I lost,
You'd find me duteous at my post ;
And up to Dublin I would trot,
And off I'd be like pistol shot
To bring the Major's fine petition,
To which I bow with great submission.
But now, alas ! I can't stir out,
Because I've got a flying gout.
Will you go, Sir Pat O'Connor ?

SIR PAT :

Not a foot upon my honour.
Barny, Barny, buck or doe,
Who shall with the petition go ?
Every one cries No, No, No !
Billy Murphy tell your reason.

BILLY MURPHY :

This is now the slaughtering season.
What do you say, Mr. Blake ?

MR. BLAKE :

I have got a belly-ache.

Pray, what say you, Mr. Brown?

MR. BROWN:

Business keeps me out of town.

*Jack-an-Apes-Squintum,* what say you?

JACK SQUINTUM:[1]

My clothes are old; I can't buy new.

Sir Thomas Esmonde, you agree?

SIR THOMAS:

Tell me first my company;
If the characters are fair
Gladly I'll your message bear.
I shall value or despise it,
As I see the men who prize it.

Mr. Costigan, Colonel Burke, Mr. Owen O'Connor, Mr. Roche, Mr. Bellew, General Farrell, Sir Thomas Burke—all decline, and the rhymer concludes thus :

THE MAJOR:

To oppression e'er a foe,
I'll with my petition go.
Oh, how I do feel indignant
At the impudence malignant
Of a Viceroy's Secretary—
A mean *hunch-backed crooked fairy ;*
A vile *crack-brained, stupid, vaunting,*
*Foppish, impotent, gallanting*
*Jack-a-dandy, who durst write*
*Letters, casting scorn and spite*
On the Catholic Committee,
Full of men both wise and witty :
Liberal men, with proper feeling,
Ne'er to priests, like *bigots,* kneeling ;
But who feel like men on matters :
Scorn the *anti-veto praters,*

---

[1] This was John Lawless ; a broad-shouldered fellow, with good brow and forehead, always putting up his glass to his eye. Wrote a History of Ireland ; was a henchman of O'Connell's.

And care not about low or high day,
Whether Christmas or good Friday.
Each should feel it much behooves him
To pray the Regent to remove him.
I will go, without delay,
Though behind the rest may stay.

The charges against the Duke of Richmond, Lord
Lieutenant, and Wellesley Pole, his Secretary, were—
that Wellesley Pole informed the Catholic Committee,
by a public letter, that the scheme of adding to the
Committee ten members (representatives, as some called
themselves,) from each county, was a breach of the
Convention Act.

Then came the making of Dr. Patrick Duigenan
(Vicar-General of so many dioceses, and a kind of
Protestant Pope), a Privy Councillor ; and the promot-
ing of Mr. Gifford, the " Dog in Office," as he was
nicknamed, to a place in the Customs.[1] But these
two men, said Dr. Brenan, could not do as much harm
as Major Bryan, who, at Kilkenny, exerted himself for
the Veto—" that infernal machine against the National
faith, opposed by the clergy and the nation."

The Duke of Richmond, said Dr. Brenan, discoun-
tenanced the Orange parades round King William's
statue in College Green, and though Mr. O'Connell
charged the Duke with passing his time between the
racket-court and whisky-punch-drinking, it no more
incapacitated him than the unwieldy elegance of a
protuberant belly improved Mr. O'Connell.

---

[1] Dr. Patrick Duigenan, LL.D. (the Right Hon.), married the widow
Hepenstal, mother of the Walking-Gallows, and of two fine young heifers
that Dr. Duigenan was proud of riding with in the Phœnix Park. Mrs.
Hepenstal dwelt at Sandymount Green. I well remember her daughters,
unmarried and old when I saw them. Jack Hepenstal dwelt, in later years,
in Stephen's Green, and had a rope ladder in the rere of his dwelling to
escape by. He feared assassination.

The Duke's athletics, said Dr. B., had one good effect at all events, viz.: that it freed the Duke and Dr. Brenan himself from having insults cast on them at a nearer distance than Talla' Hill (a hill five miles south of Dublin), whence a man insulted in the streets once challenged his opponent. Thenceforth a cowardly boaster's threats were known as " Talla' Hill talk."

Counsellor Leather-skull Jackanapes Finn (a con-nexion of O'Connell's) had called Mr. Pole a coward; out a brother of Lord Wellington's was not afraid to fight, said Dr. Brenan.

O'Connell and Finn called Wellesley Pole ugly. He had not (no doubt) the intrepidity of face (said Dr. Brenan) so admired in Mr. Finn, nor the sweet Munster smile " Caed Mille Failtha," of Kerry, which ennobled the face of Mr. O'Connell.

But all said that knew Mr. Wellesley Pole (as all said of Mr. Finn)

" His heart keeps the promise you got from his face."


" If any Catholic in Ireland (says Dr. Brenan in conclusion), has a right to complain, I am the man. Till God sent me a property the other day, I should have been liable to the charge of not having a stake in the country.

" I am the head (he continued) of the valiant family of O'Brenan, and Prince of Edough, a family that never had a Protestant in it, or a Veto-man, or a trimmer. The Earl of Strafford, Lord Lieutenant of Ireland, robbed us to enrich his cousin, Sir Christopher Wandesford, and cast us out bare on the wide world.

"In spite of successive plunderings we prospered. Never did we want an estate, and we are connected with the best Catholic blood in Ireland.

"When I see those whose ancestors were digging potatoes when my family were losing principalities,— when I see such men petitioning for the removal of Viceroys and disturbing a nation, I cannot but say ye are too hot,—and I fear the Prince Regent may say the same, and perhaps put us all upon a more cooling regimen."

Dr. Brenan describes Dr. Drumsnuffle's *Pulvis Elo-quentiæ*, or, Orators' Snuff, that enlivened the fancy and irradiated the faculties ; and his Veto Pills, that had been used by Dr. Milner and the ablest Veto Theologians. It was a medicine recommended to the Catholic bishops that insulted the Veto proposal as madness, and a gross imposition on Catholicity.

In a sale of pictures in May, 1812, " No. XII. The Storming of Fort Veto by General Milner (the Rev. Dr. Milner of Winchester), is a grand descriptive piece ; the likenesses of the Great Veto Champions are preserved (with much flattery). Major Bryan, Counsellors O'Connell, O'Gorman, Fin, Ned Hay (Secretary to the Catholic Committee), Denis Cassin, Tom Finn the currier, have justice done, to their dis-comfiture and noses."

In Dr. Brenan's " Address to the Roman Catholic Christians of Ireland " (in the Magazine for June, 1812), he says: " I have the consolation to say that I was the only man in Ireland that opposed the Veto manfully. I say I opposed it manfully,—the others in the abstract : I opposed the men and the measure. I made the upstart, who would mend Church discipline, recollect his grandfather that was mending shoes: and the consequence was, that were I not The Wrestling Doctor, and better known to the mob of Dublin than most men that Dublin ever saw, the labours of Cox, Fin, Fitzpatrick, Keelin, and Drumsnufflle would have caused the dogs of Dublin to have lapped my blood."

He launches (in December, 1814) into these rhymes against the Veto, to the tune of " Drops of Brandy :"—

> The Ascendancy men got a hope
>     That they'd settle d—d Popery's fate, O,
> Could they make our old Sovereign Pope
>     By the magical term of the Veto.
>
> For they said, though we cannot complain
>     That they make great men bishops of late, O,
> Still a Coppinger[1] may come again,
>     And we'll lay him aside by the Veto.
>
> When we once get the negative royal,
>     Each man who has brains we'll say nay to,
> And we'll pick out the stupid and loyal,
>     And mitre them up with the Veto.
>
> Mr. Wickham,[2] a politic viper,
>     Gave seven old bishops a treat, O,
> Dr. Troy got as drunk as a piper,
>     And swore that he'd give up the Veto.
>
> But when he grew sober next morn,
>     And heard the fine things he said yea to,
> He swore he'd in pieces be torn,
>     And be d—d ere he gave up the Veto.

---

[1] Dr. Coppinger was Bishop of Cloyne in 1798. He was informed by a Catholic Soldier that the Orangemen intended to murder him. But, after inquiry, he disbelieved the story. The authorities then arrested Dr. Coppinger, to make him disclose the soldier's name, but he stedfastly refused.—Canon Keller, P.P., interviewed on his release from Kilmainham. *Freeman's Journal*, Monday, May 23rd, 1887.

[2] Chief Secretary for Ireland.

Among the Veto Men satirized was Daniel O'Connell. He was the Kerry Atticus, Counsellor Roundabout from Kerry ! " In April, 1812 (writes Dr. Brenan), the city received a shock during the last week never before felt in Dublin. And, oh Heavens ! we learned at once that Counsellor O'Connell was shot in a duel ! "

" To use a newspaper phrase, the effect is easier imagined than described.

" The painter of Babylon in ruins—of Jeremy lamenting,—of Rachel weeping for the loss of her children who would not be comforted,—could not do the picture justice. This young Veto and Anti-Union Marcellus sinking under his *Aspera fata*, stretched a beauteous corpse on the couch of honour down in Tralee, the native city of Teddy Foley . . . . Dr. Drumsnuffle is said to have wept bitterly, as he knew what it was to be killed in a duel from experience . . . Ned Hay[1] bought a suit of black off the first peg in Plunket Street, the old clothes market, and went to Dr. Troy, Catholic Archbishop of Dublin, to have an ' Office ' for him, and to request that Liffey Street Chapel should be open to receive the corpse. This being refused, as unfit for a suicide and homicide combined, provoked Count Naso,[2] and he was rude, and spoke some unintelligible threats through the ruins of his nose.

"The people of Merrion Square,[3] seeing the crowds gathering, posted guards at each corner. Several

---

[1] Secretary to the Catholic Committee.

[2] " Naso," in Latin means a nose.

[3] O'Connell dwelt on the south side of the Square, three doors westward of the corner of Lower Fitzwilliam Street, where Dr. Kidd now dwells.

Catholic ladies miscarried at the fright . . . Bladder-chops was heard to say, that since he left the Bar for the Bench, there never was such a man for uncommon talents as O'Connell. Dr. Troy said, that was it not for a bias he (O'Connell) had to *Unitariunism*, he would consider him a saint. All the ladies said, that was it not for the big belly he got latterly they could embrace him as the Catholic champion. When lo! an attorney's clerk arrives from Kerry, and announces that Counsellor O'Connell is still alive and in perfect speech-making condition, and that he would soon be in Dublin and make a speech that would contain the old matter that ferments the mob and ferments every one of all his famous speeches.

" In February, 1817 (said Dr. Brenan), the Catholic Board felt (on the occasion of the treasonable Spa-fields riot in London), humbled, but not vanquished. And, not to be outdone, Mr. O'Connell and Mr. Scully, and Barny Coyle, called a meeting at Harold's Cross. Mr. O'Connell rose and smiled—a revolu-tionary smile—that won the hearts of the people. He spoke of poor Ireland and all about her. He spoke about the Catholic religion,—which he loved because it was Irish,—and the harbour of Dunleary,—and the Princess of Wales,—and the rise in the price of Congou tea,—he spoke of the ballad singers and the battle of Waterloo, and he added five thousand new grievances to the thirty-five thousand he manufactured formerly. The Counsellor exhorted them to modera-tion in eating and drinking, and in the expression of their feelings under the horrible government which loaded himself and his children with the chains of slavery. He sat down amidst thunders of applause

and cries of " O'Connell for ever "—O'Connell's industry at his profession was great.  He rose before
day.

In a poetical review of the Irish Bar, Dr. Brenan
says :—

O you, whose soft soul may detain you a-raking,
Who have spent your whole night some fool's good cheer par-
    taking,
If, on your return, you pass Merrion-square,
About five in the morning, you'll certainly stare,
Seeing light in a window and none in its neighbour,
And you'll cry, " Here's some wake or some woman in labour ! "
Although no way curious, both you and your friend
Will climb on the rails, or the steps will ascend,
And there, falling short, you will rise on your pattens,
And you'll cry, " 'Tis a Popish priest saying his matins ! "
A fine man in person, with belly so round
That you'll think 'tis some great learned bishop you've found.
But, so comely and tall, he can't be Dr. Troy,
But a man quite the model of Father Molloy ;
Which thought makes you stretch to see, if you're able,
To find is a girl hid under the table !
Then a crucifix strikes you,[1] on which fixed in thought are
His laughing blue eyes ;[2] and the blest holy water,
And scapular by it, decide you, at least,
That he must be some sanctified orthodox priest ;
And the face, that so typifies apple potato,[3]
Proclaims him an Irish priest *not for* the Veto ;
But, in turning about : Heavens ! what are you finding ?
All hell's vile artillery—law books in binding,
And law books in leaves with blue covers, and sheets ;
And vile law your vision in every shape meets.

---

[1] O'Connell had a large crucifix, so placed that it could be seen hanging
in his study from the outside of the house.

[2] One of the characteristic features of O'Connell.

[3] The " Rosy Apple " potato, of Balrothery, County Dublin, was the
choicest potato of Dublin fifty years ago.

Oh ! the guile of the heart, like the guile of the face,
an sanctify men without honour or grace !
Thus, you'll talk to yourself, and, perchance, the next day,
You espy your law crucifix, caravat-prig,
Whom you scarce recognise in a gown and a wig.
You follow him into the different courts ;
In the Pleas, like its chief or "Joe Miller," he sports
He, in Chancery, blarnies, and in *Regis Banco* [1]
He plays to Law's Quixote the Sycophant Sancho ;
In the Rolls, with MacMahon, [2] wise, sage, and demure,
He leaves all his roisterings outside the door ;
Nor into the Exchequer brings bluster and vapours,
Where O'Grady cuts up all fine cutters of capers. [3]
Go here or go there—you can't be at a loss—
To Donnybrook, Riding House, or Harold's Cross.
There he weeps as sincerely, as lately he laughed,
For Erin, unspurred, fighting England when gaffed. [4]
You retire, and, next morning, you'll pass Merrion-square,
And you'll look where the light is : The crucifix there
You espy ; and espy, in the very same place,
The man who was there with the belly and face.
And 'tis now you are sorry his name you don't know,
And to remedy this to the watchman you go. [5]
" Watch ! " you say, " Who is he I see every night
At his prayers—at his business—beyond at the light ? "
The watchman will tell you : " Though here is my station—
A poor, common watchman,—that man's my relation ;
My true born cousin, by the mother's side—
Of Munster the glory—of Kerry the pride.
I'll never deny it wherever I go,
Dan Connell's my name, but Dan takes the big O.

---

[1] Latin for King's Bench.

[2] Sir William MacMahon, Bart., Master of the Rolls.

[3] Chief Baron O'Grady, of most caustic wit.

[4] Game cocks, armed for the fight, were spurred or " gaffed " with sharp steel.

[5] The watchmen of Dublin were clad in frieze great coats, carried short half pikes, and a lanthorn. They cried the hours of the night and state of the weather : "Half-past twelve, and a starlight night."

We were reared both for clergy, but changed from that trade ;
He went to the lawyers,[1] and I to the spade."
" Past four ! " cried the watchman : " You start, 'tis so late."

  .    .    .    .    .    .    .    .    .    .

The Councillor's tall, and he's big to be sure ;
As in Kerry they say " He's the full of a door."
But indeed, to be sure, as for walking the street,
He's a *flaughoolagh* [2] body to follow or meet —
To see such congenial *prapeen* [3] all about him,
For a true-hearted Irishman no one can doubt him.
His looks—nothing cringing—no meanness betray,
But he's all *faugh-a-ballagh*—" Keep out of the way ! "
And, following him, he delights each beholder,
The umbrella thrown manfully over his shoulder
Like a pike.   He reminds us of old days of glory,
When bold Father Murphy thus marched into Gorey.
He's the wonderful Scapin [4] whose numerous feats
Enthrone him the prince of political cheats.
Indeed, in the summer they call Ninety-Eight,
When labourers were few and the harvest was great,
The reaper of laurels appeared rather fickle,
For when reaping set in he retired with his sickle,
And on his estate, in the rocks near Tralee,
Wooed the nymph of his soul whom he calls Liberty.
In those days as in these, he was not very stirring,
But left all his work to M'Nally and Curran.
When Emmet rose in Eighteen Hundred and Three,
Then no prettier Yeoman in Dublin you'd see.
This Philistine Goliath, in King's regimentals,
Astonished the Jews and confounded the Gentiles ;

---

[1] O'Connell was educated at St. Omer for the Church, and has told how,
as he and other young students walked the halls and cloisters there, they
caught (or were caught by) the Revolutionary fire of the times in France
But he afterwards asked pardon of God for this wickedness.

[2] " Flaughoolagh " is princely, open-hearted, or generous.

[3] " Prapeen," ragamuffins]

[4] The Varlet in " The Barber of Seville " who makes a tool and fool of
his Master.

And at drill in the ranks, the Orangemen callous
Admired Munster Sinon [1] was not on the gallows. [2]

[1] Sinon was the Greek who got into the belly of the Grecian horse of wood, and the horse being received into Troy, Sinon opened the city gates and let in the Greeks.

[2] This is a perfect portrait and biography for so much of O'Connell. I speak from having seen him and watched him during the last twenty years of his life.

## CHAPTER III

## DR. BRENAN AND THE DUBLIN DOCTORS.

"THE Milesian Magazine" is over-stocked with lampoons
of the medical practitioners of Dublin. In a catalogue
of the sale of Dr. Drumsnuffle's books we read as
follows : " No. II.—His state of quackery all over
the globe, and his review of psycho-chirurgical and
pharmaceutical pretenders at present in the city of
Dublin—*cum notis variorum.*" " This last work of
Dr. Drumsnuffle's," says Dr. Brenan, " is a poetic
effusion of much malice and not a little wit. Dr.
Drumsnuffle takes the doctors alphabetically. . . . .
The plan, however," adds Dr. Brenan, " is not original,
but borrowed from the poem in the ' Child's Play-
thing.' It is entitled, ' A Review of the Dublin
Doctors.'

> ' A was an archer that shot at a frog.
> B was a butcher,' &c.

" The first character he introduces," continues Dr.
Brenan, " is Dr. A., who, on the trial of Mr. Whaley,
swore very serviceably, which Doctor D. seems to
consider in an unfavourable light. We shall give his
epigram, as we may call it." (It need hardly be said
that the poetry and all are Dr. Brenan's own)—

> ' A was Archer—a Doctor of singular skill—
> He saved but one life, when he swallowed a pill.
> His patient, a man of high consequence really,[1]
> The Kill-coachee son of old Burn-chapel Whaley.

---

[1] The old fashioned pronunciation of this word in Ireland rhymes
perfectly with Whaley.

His disease, would you know, without jesting or joking,
Was *Cynanche legalis*, that kills men by choking.[1]
And such was the pill which he swallowed whole as,
Would be unto Jemmy O'Brien a bolus.

The Whaleys owned great estates in the counties
of Galway, Wicklow, Armagh, and Dublin, derived
from the Cromwellian Era.[2]

Cornet Richard Whaley, founder of the Whaley
family, was grandson to Edward Whaley the Regicide,
a first cousin of Oliver Cromwell's, who only escaped

---

[1] Cynanche (pronounced Kynanche) is Quinsy. *Cynanche legalis*, is death by hanging for murder, alluding to Colonel William Whaley being tried for the murder of James Purcell, the hackney coachman. The pill must have reference to Dr. Archer's evidence in favour of Colonel William Whaley, which, Dr. Brenan suggests, would hardly have been dared to be given by Jemmy O'Brien. Jemmy O'Brien was one of the Informers of '98, called by Curran the battalion of testimony, and was himself at length hanged. The government could make no use of Jemmy O'Brien's evidence after Curran's cross-examination of him in 1798. But he was still kept by Major Sirr as a spy. In 1800 there was a football match in a walled field at Kilmainham. The Major, taking Jemmy O'Brien and a body of soldiers with him, bade O'Brien stay with some soldiers at one gate while he went with others to a second gate. O'Brien got over the wall instead. The people cried out, "O'Brien the informer," and ran, all but a poor, decrepit man that O'Brien stabbed to the heart with a dagger. For this he was hanged. When the wretched Jemmy O'Brien was about to be executed he exhibited the greatest terror, and lingered at his devotions to thus protract his life for a few minutes. "Tom Galvin," the hangman, who was always impatient of any delay by his victims, called out at the cell door so as to be heard by O'Brien and all the bystanders—"Mr. O'Brien, jewel! Long life to you! Make haste wid' your prayers—the people's getting tired waiting so long under de swing-swong."

"Ireland Sixty Years Ago." M'Glashan. Dublin, 1847. Re-issued by M. H. Gill & Son, Dublin, under the title of "Ireland Ninety Years Ago," n 1885. Both Works 12mo.

Jemmy O'Brien's appearance on the scaffold was hailed with a shout of savage exultation by the mob.

[2] See two very interesting genealogical papers by W. F. Littledale, Esq., Solicitor, of "The Cottage," Whaley Abbey, Rathdrum, Co. Wicklow, in "Notes and Queries," in No. 78, June 26, 1869; and No. 128, 10th June, 1576.

the dreadful death awarded to traitors by flying to America, where he died after seven years of hardship, hiding in woods and caves.

Edward Whaley the regicide had a brother Henry Whaley. He sat as Member of Parliament for Peebles-shire and Selkirkshire in Cromwell's United Parliament at Westminster. He came over to Ireland, and as an Adventurer got lands in the County of Galway, and was made Judge Advocate General of the Army in Ireland. He became a zealous Royalist, and in the Convention of February, 1660, moved the resolution for recalling the King. He sat in the Irish Parliament for Athenry. He lost lands to the value of £20,000 restored to the Earl of Clanricarde; and at the dissolution in 1666, was recommended by Parliament to the care of the Duke of Ormonde for his services in the Convention and his losses, as appears by the Duke's letter of 15th August, 1666, to the Commissioners of the Court of Claims.[1]

Henry's only son, John Whaley, married Susanna, daughter (as appears by her Petition) of the principal dry nurse to the King and to four more of his Majesty's brothers and sisters. A Bill for his compensation (she says) was prepared, but never passed, because of the dissolution. As there were two Bonds of £200 each due by her husband in the Exchequer, she prayed the King to relieve him as he was unable to discharge them, which Ormonde, on being referred to, recommended.[2]

Cornet Richard Whaley married the daughter of Richard Chappel of Armagh, whence the name of

---

[1] C. P. cxliv. 88. See also Lord Mountmorres's History of the Irish Parliament from 1634 to 1660, Vol. 2, p. 159.

[2] Petition of Susanna Whaley, with Ormonde's note pursuant to H. M.'s reference of 23rd September, 1668. C. P. clx. 14.

Chappel Whaley. Richard Whaley had a son by Elizabeth Chappel called Richard Chappel, after himself, who married his cousin Susanna Whaley, and this last-named pair were parents of Thomas (the celebrated " Buck Whaley ") and of Colonel William Whaley, his youngest brother, called " Kill-coachee " in Dr. Brenan's rhymes. It was " Buck Whaley" that for a bet of £20,000 or £30,000 undertook to walk from Dublin to Jerusalem and back within the year. He must have set out in 1788, for there is an extract from a letter from Smyrna, of December 2, 1788, saying:—"I have seen Mr. Whaley, Mr. Moore of the 18th Regt. of Foot, and Mr. Wilson. They are going to Jerusalem to decide a bet of £30,000 which Mr. Whaley has laid with the Duke of Leinster, Lord Drogheda, and some others."[1]

" On Saturday the 6th of July, 1789, his presence in London is noted in the ' Gentleman's Magazine ;' and, in the same work, his return to Dublin on 26th of July in the same year is recorded, and his winning of his bet.

" The writer mentions that Richard Chappel Whaley, the 'Buck's' father, was active as a Magistrate in Ireland during the Scotch Rebellion of 1745, and fired a shot one day that set fire to the thatch of a Roman Catholic Chapel, and the people of the neighbourhood nick-named him from this circumstance 'Burn-chapel Whaley.'

" His youngest son, Colonel William, got the name of ' Kill-coachee ' from the following circumstance :— On the 18th of May, 1791, he hired a hackney coach to drive him from the Rotunda to his house in Denzille Street, and paid James Purcell, the owner and

[1] " Universal Magazine " for May, 1789.

driver, 1s. 7½d., his fare ; but Purcell pretended to
think the money bad, and Colonel Whaley took it back,
went in, and shut the hall-door. Purcell thereupon
kept knocking, and Whaley told him to begone, and
then came down and with a knotted stick beat him,
and charged him on the police, though Purcell said,
' After what you have given me, you might let me go
home with my coach.' He died that day week. Dr.
Clement Archer, who examined the corpse lying on
straw in Purcell's lodgings in New Street (off the
·Coombe), found head, lungs, and kidneys, without
marks of beating, and believed James Purcell died of
putrid fever, then rife in the neighbourhood. To
examine the body he had to take off as many waist-
coats as the grave-diggers in the Play of Hamlet. The
Jury in three minutes acquitted Whaley.[1]

"It was the 'Buck's' father who in 1754 built
Whaley House on the South side of Stephen's Green.
It is of Cut stone with Portico, the Portico on a high
flight of stone steps, and on the entablature a Sleeping
Lion.

" It is said that the ' Buck ' betted he would leap out
of the window over the Lion and a carriage standing
at the door. He did so. But in spite of a feather
bed laid beyond the carriage broke his leg. Some
say it was from the window of Daly's Club House in
College Green he leaped.

" Colonel William Whaley was one of the Prince
Regent's pals. In 1803 he went to France, and was
there detained among other 'Detenus' by the First
Napoleon. He was imprisoned first in the prison of

---

[1] "Dublin Chronicle." October, 1791.

L'Abbaye at Paris, afterwards at Verdun and the
fortress of Bitche, and was not released until 1814 on
the fall of Napoleon. He died at Whaley Abbey,
near Rathdrum, Co. Wicklow, 26th March, 1843 "
(Information by W. F. Littledale, May, 1887).

In " The Milesian Magazine," for 1825, under the
head " Medical Intelligence," Dr. B. satirizes Dr. Litton,
Dr. " Whisky " Bredon, Dr. Beattie, Dr. Percival, Dr.
Stoker (whose real name, according to Brenan, was
Stroker, and who was tried before Judge Bladderchops
for dropping the "r" for a very peculiar reason), and
Surgeon-General Crampton.

Dr. Brenan has the following satirical remarks on
the medical practice of that day :—

" The croton oil is doing wonders for Mrs. Farrell,
the coffin-woman in Cook-street. Paddy Rooney's
death,[1] she said, had ruined her family ; and prussic
acid was only tried seventy times by the young and
old doctors when it was cried down. ' What,' says
Mrs. Farrell, ' is seventy lousy coffins to what I made
of Mills[2] by bleeding in fevers ? May Heaven be
Dr. Mills' bed when he dies a Papist (as I'm told the
Ranelagh nuns and Prince Hohenlohe pray and say he
will). I'm sure I'd be ungrateful if I begrudged him
the best coffin in the shop. Long life to you Dr.
Mills ; but I'll bury you like a friend and a gentleman
whenever you die ! Long life to you, but I'll cover
your coffin with angels in real block tin !

" The late Mrs. Corbally, of prussic acid memory, was
a woman greatly afraid of a lingering death. She made
a ' Novena,' that is a prayer of sixteen hours a day on

---

[1] One of the Dublin doctors.
[2] A Protestant physician.

her bare knees, and fasted from milk in her tea and from windows cut on her bread and butter. She sent a fee of two hogs,[1] as a German, to Prince Hohenlohe, requesting his advice upon the shortest mode of going soon and suddenly to heaven. His letter ran thus in autograph, which is framed and glazed in Ranelagh Nunnery[2]:—

> Si regnum cœli
> Vult adire Corbeeli.
> Citò adsit princeps
> Medicorum ; déinceps
> Huic est medicamen
> Malorum levamen.

" Her confessor, Father Dandy Henery, told her the ' prince of doctors ' was Crampton, the Surgeon Barber ; and the dandy translated this elegant Latin epistle in the following manner :—

> The holy Prince of Hohenlohe
> Hereby doth let the lady know
> That, if she gets the prussic acid,
> He knows not what did e'er surpass it.
> Most quickly she'll return to dust ;
> If God don't have her the devil must.
> But this point she'll feel no trouble in,
> When Beelzebub knows she's from Dublin.
> Without the passport of a sin
> The devil must let the lady in.
> If he refuses, let me know,—
> Your humble servant,—HOHENLOHE.

In the year 1823, Prince Hohenlohe caused a commotion in the world by some extraordinary cures—

---

[1] A " hog " was the slang word for a shilling.
[2] Ranelagh is a suburb of Dublin, on the South side.

miraculous, as was alleged by his supporters, amongst whom may be accounted the celebrated "J. K. L.," or John Bishop of Kildare and Leighlin—no less celebrated for his political writings than for his acute investigation of pretended apostolic powers. Mr. W. J. Fitzpatrick, in his "Life of the Right Rev. Dr. Doyle,"[1] says "the three ablest opponents whom Doyle encountered were the Surgeon-General (Sir Philip Crampton, Bart.), Baron Smith and Dr. Cheyne."[2] But so great was the controversy that, in the Haliday Collection of pamphlets in the Royal Irish Academy, there are four volumes of the year 1823, each containing a dozen pamphlets and more.[3] To give the title of one—"A Pastoral Address and a Correspondence between the Right Rev. Dr. Doyle, Roman Catholic Bishop of Kildare and Leighlin, and His Serene Highness the Rev. Prince Hohenlohe of Bamber, on a most extraordinary miracle wrought by His Highness on a young Lady in the Queen's County who was dumb for several years. Dublin: M'Mullen and Co., South George's Street, 1823. Price 5d." Dr. Murray, Roman Catholic Archbishop of Dublin, also issued a Pastoral on the miraculous cure of Mrs. Mary Stuart, a Religieuse of the Convent of St. Joseph, Ranelagh, with certificates of Dr. Mills, Dr. Cheyne, Surgeon MacNamara, and the affidavits of Mrs. Mary Stuart, Mrs. Ann Stuart, Catherine Hosey, Mrs Margaret Dillon, Mrs. Margaret Lynch, the Rev. John Meagher, and the Rev. Charles Stuart. Published by Richard Coyne, Capel Street, Printer and Publisher to the Royal College, Maynooth. 1823.

[1] James Duffy, Wellington-quay, Dublin, 1861., 2 Vols. 8vo.
[2] Ibid. I. 246.
[3] The volumes are bound and are numbered 1267, 1268, 1269, 1270.

There is much humour in the reports of trials before Judge Bladderchops—the doctor's very appropriate name for Lord Norbury. He gives an etching of the Court of Common Pleas, as frontispiece to the case of "The Lying-in Hospital *versus* Dr. Brenan," in his Magazine for December, 1813, with a likeness, as he informs his readers, of the " Wrestling Doctor" (and his big stick, he might have added,) and of Norbury, of the wigged barristers, and of the jury. Some of these " Reports" use too plain language for the taste of the present day. In the Magazine for July, 1812, is " The trial of John Gilmore, a Popish priest, for wearing a Protestant hat contrary to His Majesty's Crown an. .dignity, &c., &c."

Counsellor Slow, in his opening speech, said he felt the weight of the present prosecution, as one that involved their dearest rights—their religious immunities. John Gilmore, a Popish Priest, had been apprehended in the very act of wearing a Protestant hat through the streets of Dublin and upon the King's highway. The offence was made capital without benefit of clergy by the 52nd of Henry VIII., where it is enacted (continued Counsellor Slow) that any man professing the Popish religion, who shall counterfeit the guise of a Protestant shall suffer death without benefit of clergy. [The trial proceeds] :—

Call Justice Drury,[1] who is sworn.—Had information against the prisoner, and arrested him.

---

[1] Justice Drury halted in his gait, and hence was styled " Lame Justice." On the occasion of Robert Emmet's insurrection, in 1803, he retired for safety to his house in the Coombe, from whence, as Curran remarked, "he played with considerable effect on the rebels with a large telescope."—" Ireland Sixty Years Ago."

### Cross-examined by Mr. Beetle.

Pray, Mr. Drury, on what charge did you arrest the prisoner ?

*Drury*—Upon the charge of wearing a Protestant hat.

*Beetle*—What do you call a Protestant hat ?

*Drury*—I call any hat that I'm told is a Protestant hat.

*Beetle*—Is that a Protestant hat (*showing Counsellor Slow's hat*) ?

*Drury*—No, Sir. That I call a fool's cap.

[Whoever the cap fits let him wear it,—*from the Bench.*]

*Beetle*—Mr. Drury : By virtue of your oath, do you not believe that the prisoner at the bar wore that believing it to be a genuine Roman Catholic and Apostolic hat ?

*Drury*—No, sir ! No man could have worn that hat but for the basest purposes of High Treason and of overturning our happy Constitution.

*Beetle*—Mr. Drury, how much would you take to swear that hat is Lord Norbury's wig ?

*Counsellor Slow*—Don't answer the question ! It is irrelevant ! I appeal to the Bench.

*Beetle*—Go down, Mr. Drury.


### Dr. Paddy Paddereen sworn.

Had information from a priest that that fellow at the bar was in the habit of wearing a Reformation or Thirty-Nine Article hat ; felt it his duty to have him arrested ; he owned he wore the hat as a Protestant hat.

*Cross-examined by Counsellor M'Limpy.*

Pray, doctor, did you hold out any hope or threat to him when he owned it was a Protestant hat ?

A.—No.

Q.—Did he freely confess it was a Protestant hat ?

A.—Yes.

Q.—Pray, now, do you think if he was aware that it was really a Protestant hat he would confess it ?

A.—I don't know what a blackguard Popish priest would confess. I believe they would say or swear anything.

Q.—Pray, doctor, have you examined the hat ?

A.—I have.

Q.—What is it that makes the difference in the two hats ?

A.—The cock.

Q.—Then am I to understand that a Roman Catholic 'Popish hat has a bigger cock or a smaller cock than a Protestant hat ?

A.—Sir, you seem to know nothing of the law of cocks ! The hat, at the blessed Reformation, was made the type and figure of the Head of the Church. Henry the Eighth was figured as the top or head of the body Ecclesiastic, or Church, by the hat ; and the hat was made to typify still further the blessed founder and royal author of our reformed faith by its modelling or configuration. Each Protestant divine was to stand up and show the faith that was in him by the cock in his hat. It was then made felony for any Popish priest to meddle with this article of religion, and if any priest dared to cock his hat he was to do it in private under pain of death.

## Mr. Fin, the hatter.

Is a Protestant hat-maker ; knows the cock of ecclesiastical hats, and the difference between a bishop's, rector's, and curate's cock. Made the hat of the prisoner at the bar, and sold it to him as a Protestant hat with a dean's cock.

The Judge here summed up the evidence with his usual perspicacity, says Dr. Brenan, and dwelt on the smallest particle of the case. We cannot follow him through the whole. But, in substance, the charge was as follows :—" Gentlemen,—I need not deal with you, as is the custom in ordinary cases, and with ordinary men. Happy is the man that feels himself convicted by such a set of men. It must console him to think that if he was to go to the gallows he bore to it such a passport as your verdict. The prisoner at the bar, from his extraordinary talents (for I hear that Billy MacDonnell says he is a man of prodigious acquirements), must have had some more than ordinary view of the heinous imposture of which he is about to be found guilty. When the clergy assume preposterous habiliments, let the State look to it ! When high dignitaries of the Church wear web pantaloons,[1] though the daughters of Jerusalem may rejoice, let

---

[1] Dr. Brenan has the following "Impromptu" on a reverend dandy gentleman who was neither clad like Solomon in all his glory, nor like the lily of the field, nor like a Freemason, nor like Adam and Eve when fig-leaved after sin :—

*Nudus agas ; minùs est insania turpis.*
(Go naked—madness might then be some excuse.)

Doff thy net-covers, and strut in thy skin,
By madness absolved from all crime and all sin ;
Nor as now, when we start at the gauze pantaloon,
Shall we blush that you can't plead the full of the moon.

the Sanhedrim look to it ! But when Popish priests reveal an open hostility to all that is lovely in the Constitution, by pointing the cocks of their hats against social order and religion, it is time to exclaim, ' The Church and State are in danger !' This man has called men to his character. I expected Dr. Troy.[1] For my part, I feel divested of prejudice as much as the case admits of ; but I do not see how the unhappy man can get over the indictment."

The jury found him guilty without leaving the box. The Judge sentenced him as follows :—

" John Gilmore, I am happy to tell you that if ever a man got a fair trial you are the man. A jury of your countrymen has found you guilty of a crime that has begun with you, and, I hope, will end where it began. The law makes the crime death without benefit of clergy ; but the law should have said with benefit to clergy ; for, if you could run your cocked hat into the society of privileged men, as to cocks and hats, the Lord help them ! I hope you will not think me severe if I order you to be taken from the place whence you came, and, on Saturday next, hung till you are dead as a cock at the front of the jail,—and I wish you a very good morning."

The following are some of Dr. Brenan's epigrams :

" On Loyal Sam Coates, of Beresford's Yeomanry Corps":—" Few men of incorrupt manners have suffered more from evil communications than John Claudius Beresford. Into his most respectable corps some prime ruffians made their way, and brought disgrace on it and its commander. Chief in that

---

[1] The Most Rev. Dr. Troy was, at that time, Roman Catholic Arch-bishop of Dublin.

M

number was John Burke, *alias* Tipperary Fitzsimmons,
and Sam Coates. The former has long since been
transported out of the Revenue to Botany Bay. The
latter has gone across the water for robbery. Sam
did not travel without the notice of minstrelsy. We
must first give some of the last public acts of this
great functionary. 'Loyal Sam Coates.' Tune—
' Clever Tom Clinch.' "

This song deplores (says Dr. Brenan) the fate of
one of the most loyal defenders of the Constitution in
1798. He was chief in the famous battle of Rath-
farnham under Tipperary Fitzsimmons, where six foot-
passengers and a fool were vanquished by the Riding
House Army,[1] and hanged in a cow-house ! When
half dead, Sam Coates showed great humanity, for he
put them out of pain by " buttering his sword in their
guts,"—his own happy expression.

" When loyal Sam Coates found his stags unavailing,
And convicted he stood of portmanteau-stealing,
He turned to the boys in the dock that were lagged,
And he cried, ' Devil thank them,—'tis well we're not scragged.'
I flogged, murdered, robbed in the year Ninety-Eight,
And I got great applause. Is all law changed of late ?
While for comical murders such credit I bore,
They called me ' *Joe Miller* ' in Beresford's corps.
Well, zounds, when I'm landed in Botany Bay,
I wonder what will all the vagabonds say !
They'll think I came there, I'll lay any wager,
As a Government spy, or a friend of the Major ;[2]
For how can they think that the laws are so altered,
That an Orangeman can be transported or haltered ?

----

[1] It was in the Riding House attached to Tyrone (or Beresford) House,
in Marlborough-street, now the abode of the Commissioners of National
Education that the Croppies were continually a-flogging, in 1798, by the
Beresford Corps.
[2] Major Sirr, who arrested Lord Edward Fitzgerald.

I who, when Macan I saw hanging, have said
' God damn 'em, why are they so long with his head ?' [1]
And, turning to Armstrong Jemmy,[2] my neighbour
Said, ' Damn me but I'll cut it off with my sabre.'
Well, boys, sure it's hard that I must leave a nation
Where I murdered and robbed to effect its salvation.
But since law, like necessity, all must obey,
Damn Ireland ;—And here goes to Botany Bay ! "

[1] The disembowelling before the culprit in treason was quite dead, and burning his private parts, and his bowels, in his view, being given up, the beheading was retained.

[2] Captain James Armstrong, of King's County Militia, who entrapped the two Sheareses, barristers, hanged in 1798.

## CHAPTER IV

## EPITAPHS BY DR. BRENAN.

DR. BRENAN conveyed the cruellest satires in epitaphs.

### EPITAPH ON FITZMONKEY.

Here lies Fitzmonkey,—son of old Tipperary—
Whose greatest sin was that he was a fairy.
He was a counsellor, and wore a wig;
And gave opinions which were worth a fig.
He ne'er paid a penny of what he borrowed,
And, at his death, the huxter women sorrowed.
　　His soul, I'm sure, doth now repose in glory;
　　If not in hell, just try in purgatory.


### EPITAPH ON FATHER HALY.

Here lies, very gaily, the good Father Haly,
The parish priest of Castlecomer,
Who never read one word of Homer,
Nor ever talked of worldly news,
But preached devoutly upon dues.
His appetite was orthodox
Concerning bacon, hens, and cocks.
His charity to every sinner
Was great who asked him to a dinner.
In short, as long as he was able,
He fought the d—l at the table;
And when he found he lost his seat,
He'd rather tumble than retreat.
This good Apostle got a cholic,
Which turned out a dying frolic:
And when he found his hour was near,
He took a double dose of beer.
He died, but, gracious heaven be thanked,
He got himself well signed and franked,[1]

---

[1] It was the privilege of all Members of Parliament to " frank " (or mail free of postage) by their signatures a certain number of letters every day.

And, in the post-box safely thrown,
To Heaven to journey all alone;
Where to arrive he cannot fail,
Unless the D——l rob the mail.

This is an allusion to the constant robberies of the mail coaches at the period of the epitaph, which was in 1812. It was in this year that the Galway mail was received, at the Hill of Cappagh, not far from Dangan in Meath, by a gang with vollies from each side of the road. The guard fell dead. The turnpike-gate was tied. The coach passengers were robbed, and the mail bags, supposed to contain money for the approaching fair of Ballinasloe, were carried to Dangan, once the ancestral seat of the Wellesleys, but then the ɪ̇ bode of Roger O'Connor. Roger was tried for the ꞓrime of employing the gang, but was acquitted. Subsequent events led to the belief that he was the author of the robbery and murder.

EPITAPH ON CHARLEY JALAP.

*" De mortuis nil nisi bonum."*
When scoundrels die let all bemoan 'em.

Here planted like a grain of wheat or barley,—
But ne'er to vegetate,—lies Dr. Charley ;
For where would death and desolation stop
If Charley Jalap grew into a crop ?
The sexton's glory,—the gravedigger's pride—
The coffin market fell when Charley died.
With bolus, blister, vomit, purge and pill,
Did he, unceasing, Charon's wherry fill.
His powerful pills, his gasping patients owned,
By them sore pelted, like St. Stephen stoned.
His art o'erstocked the Empire of old Nick ;
The well he sickened, and he killed the sick.

## CHAPTER V.

### THE HERESY-PORTER AND THE CATHOLIC BOARD.

SOME exception, it seems, was taken to Guinness's porter as being the production of a Protestant brewer (Arthur Guinness), and secretly intended, according to Dr. Brenan's satire, to undermine the Catholic Faith, had it not been for the Catholic Board, who appointed Dr. Drumsnuffle to investigate this secret attack and analyse the porter. First, he examined several patients who had drunk of this heresy-porter, and found in them an inclination to gravity and to singing praises of the Lord through the nose. Work-men and others who indulged in it were infected with the *suspiria pia*, or holy sobbing after the Lord,—the true swaddling symptoms of stationary grace. The doctor analysed a hogshead of this anti-Popery or Counter-petition porter, and found a precipitate pro-duced by the custom, so long winked at by the Catholic Church and the Committee, of allowing swaddling porter brewers to mash up stereotype Pro-testant bibles and Methodist hymn-books in the keeve, thus impregnating, in the fermentation, the volatile parts of the porter with the ethereal essence of heresy. This brewery, since the year 1728, is said to have consumed, said Dr. Brenan, in this contraband trade 136,000 tons of bibles, and 501,000 cart-loads of hymn-books and Protestant catechisms. There happily appeared an antidote to this heresy-porter in Pim's ale. At the Rev. Dr. Troy's dinner-party, on Friday, there was, says Dr. Brenan, a select party of the clergy and the leading men of the Catholic Com-

mittee. Counsellor Bull-Stag (Denys Scully of the
" Penal Laws ") and Counsellor Roundabout from
Kerry (Daniel O'Connell), were among the company.
Dr. Troy had the ill-manners,—the illiberality,—to
have nothing but fish. It produced spasms in the
company, and Dr. Drumsnuffle was called in. To
renovate his patients he had recourse to a copper can
that stood near, but hastily cried out, " Treason,
treason,—Guiness's porter !" The company were in
horrors ! Dr. Drumsnuffle got pen, ink, and paper,
and wrote the following prescription :—" R. Cerevisi
Ricardi Pim, Quakeri, gallonias tres utatur.—S. Drum,
M.D."—[*i.e.* : Take of Dick Pim's, the Quaker's, ale,
three gallons.] The company all recovered, and Dr.
Drum favoured them with a song, of which the sixth
and last stanza is as follows :—

> To be sure you did hear of the heresy beer
>     That was made for to poison the Pope ;
> To hide the brewer a sin is,
> And his name is Arthur Guinness ;
>     For salvation he never can hope.
> But the liquor of all liquors
> That parsons, priests, and vicars—
> Saints, Swaddlers, Deists, Papists can regale ;
>     And which charms all the city,
>     And the Catholic Committee,
> And the world and its mother—is Pim's ale.

## Chapter VI

### Some Poetical Pieces by the Wrestling Doctor.

The "Widow Malone" that follows will recall
Burns' "Jolly Beggars." But in Burns the Caird (or
Tinker) prevails over his rival, the pigmy fiddle-scraper,
and other suitors for the love of "Posie Nancy," their
hostess, while the bagpiper carries off the Widow
Malone from the butcher and attorney, the bagpiper's
rivals, for her love.

#### THE WIDOW MALONE.

A landlady lived in Athlone
Who weighed to the ground twenty stone,
    She kept the "Black Boy,"
    Was an armful of joy,
And was called the sweet Mrs. Malone, och hone,
    And the beautiful Widow Malone.

Her customers, numerous grown,
Was each, as a sweetheart, well known,
    And they drank the whole year,
    In whisky and beer,
The health of sweet Widow Malone, och hone,
    And their service to Widow Malone.

A butcher, called Tom Marrabone,
Swore she should not long lie alone ;
    But her heart he did feel
    Was as hard as his steel,
And he could not get Widow Malone, och hone,
    And he had no chance of Widow Malone.

An attorney, with heart made of stone
The force of her charms did own :
    He served notice of trial,
    But got a denial
From beautiful Widow Malone, och hone.
    "Oh, I know you," says Widow Malone.

But a piper, who came from Shinrone,
Pulled out both his bag and his drone ; [1]
    He made a bold stroke,
    And he played the " Black Joke,"
And encored it for Widow Malone.

Next morning before the sun shone
She sent for old Father M'Kone,
    Who well knew his trade,
    And he very soon made
Mrs. Squeezebag of Widow Malone, och hone ;
    And now there's no Widow Malone.

Nothing has ever been written more in the style of
Mrs. Frances Harris's Petition to their Excellencies, the
Earls of Berkeley and Galway, Lords Justices of Ireland, in A.D. 1700, by Dean Swift, than the following :—

MRS. MILLS THE MIDWIFE'S LETTER TO DR. BRENAN.

Lying-in Hospital, *Feb. 1st*, 1810.

Well, Dr. Brenan, there's one thing I'd wish to say to you, and
    when I say it perhaps you'll think I'm a fool ;
And do you know what it is ?  It is this, that I think you want
    still to go to school.
To be sure I'm only a poor woman that may be out of this before
    night ;
But did you ever hear me say or do anything but what was right.
I have kept my tongue in my cheek, while I heard people talk
    about things they knew nothing about ;
But little said is soon mended, for in the end the butter will come
    out of the stirabout.
As for the business of the Women, sure they were dying by
    dozens in the hospital, just like rotten sheep ;
Till you and I put our heads together and gave that white thing
    in the bottle, but the secret you couldn't keep.

---

[1] The two principal parts of the bagpipe,—the bag to supply wind ; the
drone, with finger-holes, to give the various music notes.

Couldn't you get it, and say nothing, and let them take it just
    like burnt spirits, or anything in that way ;
And when they'd be cured let them talk about the matter, and
    "that I'm alive though I got nothing" is all they could say.
Why, my dear, you'd make your fortune if you managed the
    matter right and took them easy ;
Not to go attack that booby Ferguson, and that silly old creature,
    Dr. Hopkins, and make them crazy.

Since they all began to laugh when you said you would under-
    take their disorder to cure ;
Because not one of them ever saw anyone recover, when their
    bellies swelled, no more than I did myself, I'm sure.
But who are they but a set of jackeens, little apothecaries boys,
    and young surgeons, that it is a shame,
Never one of them came about a poor woman; but it is the
    governors alone you have to blame.
Sure so old Hopkins gets the money for the pupils, he does not
    care if they all went to Old Nick ;
Wouldn't I have died there myself, only you brought a bottle to
    me the time I was sick.
And Lady Domvile's maid, when she heard you and I talking,
    made the remark,
That the disorder we cured—both of us—was what killed her
    mistress, though she had the great Dr. Clarke.
I'd tell you what, they are all the meanest, most ignorantest, low-
    lived, jealous fellows ;
And what else could you expect, that knows no more than the man
    that came here to mend the bellows.
But if you'd keep away from the wrestling and going up to the
    Broadstone ;[1]
By my soul you'd soon show the people what would make the
    doctors cry, Och hone.

And I'd be glad you'd say nothing about the Foundling Hospital,
    or poor Dr. Harvey ;
Because the poor old man is dying, and I knew his cook, her name
    is Nell Garvey.

[1] The place where now stands the Midland Great Western Railway of
Ireland's Terminus.

But old Hopkins is coming up stairs, and I must go and give the Women a few of the House pills.[1]

And no more at present, from your friend—LUCINA TEREBINTHINA MILLS.[2]

[1] On Sunday, 13th of June, 1886, on on annual visit I pay to my friends the tenants of Viscount Clifden's lands, called Derringtanny and Clondaleebeg, in the parish of Killyon, barony of Moyfenrath, and county of Meath, the agency of which I gave up in 1852, there came down in the same train with me Dr. R. H. Fleming of the Rotunda Lying-in Hospital, a professional visit to the young wife of Thomas, son of Patrick, son of James Connolly of Derringtanny. Dr. Fleming told me that child-bed fever is now banished as an epidemic from the Lying-in Hospital owing to a system of scrupulous cleanliness enforced by Dr. Arthur V. Macan, the head of the Hospital, in walls, floors, beds and bedding—patients and attendants, doctors and pupils.

[2] "Lucina" was one of the names of Diana, the goddess, that presided over child-birth. "Terebinthina" is derived from Terebinth, the botanical name of the plant that produces turpentine.

## CHAPTER VII

## DR. BRENAN ON THE ATTORNEYS.

IT has been shown by Dr. Brenan's letter to the Chancellor, Lord Manners, that he bore a mortal hatred to Robert Cornwall, for to him he attributed (possibly unjustly) the forced and fraudulent sale of the paternal property of the Brenan family in t Castle and Castle Hill at Carlow.[1]  Dr. Bren extended his hatred from Robert Cornwall, Ned Balí and Tom Day, to the whole profession of the law— barristers as well as attorneys.  In his " Poetical review of the Irish Bar," from which the portrait of O'Connell is taken.[2]

"Now you have what I never heard called the sweet Four Courts,
    Which with Balfe, my attorney, I found very Sore Courts ;
    And, indeed, gentle reader, the same you will say,
    If you knew Neddy Balfe and (God rest him) Tom Day."

Dr. Brenan thus mentions in his Obituary of the " Milesian Magazine " for June, 1812, the death of Cornwall :—

" At his seat, Myshall Lodge,[3] Robert Cornwall, Esq., late member of Parliament for the borough of Enniscorthy—

"He was a man, take him for all in all,
    We shall not look upon his like again."

[1] See page 147, antè.
[2] Page 161, antè.
[3] Myshall is a parish in the northern part of the county of Wexford, in barony of Forth.  The village and church of Myshall stands midway on a line (imaginary) drawn between the picturesque town of Newtownbarry, on the river Slaney on the east, and Bagnalstown.  Myshall is about ten miles distance from each.

Firmly attached to our happy Constitution, in Church and State, he resisted every movement that faction ever made against our dearest rights. His name will long be remembered in the County of Carlow by the loyal and the good, whilst the rebel and the traitor shall embalm his memory in their execration. Finding that his professional pursuits, as an attorney, interfered with his permanent duties to his sovereign, he quitted that Society for the profession of arms, and, in the profession of Yeoman-Captain, he opened the free quarters campaign in Carlow and its vicinity, and, by the confiscation plan of disaffected property (thus) —so politicly adopted after him by the tyrant of Europe,—he banished treason and haberdashery from the shops and houses of the enemies of the Constitution. That calumny which ever pursues great men dogged him in his retreat from active loyalty; but he used to console himself in the words of Horace that he applied to himself,—

" ——Mens conscia recti,
Nil conscire sibi, nullâ pallescere culpâ,"

which he translated,—

" I never felt my conscience blame me,
Nor ever found an action shame me."

" It may not be amiss for the consolation of men (continues Dr. Brenan) in like circumstances as Cornwall, to mention facts illustrative of the ingratitude which great men have met with from their native country. After all Mr. Cornwall's services to the State, Lord Clare avowed from his judgment-seat in Chancery, upon a complaint made to him by one Dr. Brenan, that he (Lord Clare) would make this great

man a public example ; and the following poem
appeared calumniating his reputation : —

#### Sonnet to R. C.

Bob ! Thou shalt have a verse to make it known,
    That you're a full fraught scoundrel, pilf'ring knave ;
    Though you yourself the information gave,
To those hard fortune in your way has thrown,
For what was their's you basely made your own."

    . . . . . . . . . . .

In the previous number of the " Magazine" will be
found the following Epitaph " On Robert Cornwall,
the Attorney ":—

Beneath lies Robert Cornwall,
Whom all men did a scoundrel call—
A vile attorney, plundering yeoman,
Whose soul rapacious spared no man.
    A life embracing every sin.
And if a pound came with a curse,
He'd find a sack too small a purse.
A body gnawed with life's disease,
Showed how he toiled in Satan's ways ;
And if *he* is not lodged in Hell,
Where the Devil's Barrabas none can tell.

Dr. Brenan had an (imaginary) society for convert-
ing Irish attorneys, like Wilberforce's for the conver-
sion of the Jews.  Wilberforce's had a success (said
Dr. Brenan) that was only equalled by the ridicule
which the project had at its onset to encounter.  The
English had the glory of originating this great enterprise—a Wellingtonian enterprise we may call it—for
the promise of Sir Arthur Wellesley to drive every
Frenchman beyond the Pyrenees was deemed as fully
Quixotic as the hope uttered by Mr. Wilberforce, to
see the faithful of St. Paul's incommoded by the

press of deserters from the Synagogue. Yet this too had its fulfilment ; for not less than 30,000 old clothes-men and rag-dealers, of the Jewish caste, are now chorusing the Lord through England in the ranks of the army of the Lord of Hosts, in the life everlasting cohorts of swaddling. . . .

.     .     .     .     .     .     .

The great Dr. Drum·,[1] when the committee business[2] became slack, . . . sallied out and preached against *Latitat* and *Subpœna*[3] without ceasing. He began at the corner of Mass Lane.     .     .     .
He thence won his way (or the way of the Lord) to the very bosom of iniquity—the Hall of the Four Courts—where the word was profitable to John Scott Molloy, Sam Eastwood, Nat Montgomery, Frency Walpole, Grab Dwyer, Whelp Fitzmonkey, Kite-vulture Fearon, and a numerous herd of the *Latitat* order were smitten. They returned home weeping ; tore all their bills of costs ; burnt all their *Latitats* ; and wept over the past possession of the devil. In conclusion, said Dr. Brenan, the Doctor has got so far that he has made a select committee of the anti-robbery converts. Much is expected from this happy association·

[1] Dr. Drumsnuffle.
[2] The Catholic Committee.
[3] "Latitat" and "subpœna" are the names of writs issued in law proceedings.

"The Milesian Magazine" was also "The Irish
Monthly Gleaner ;" but it appeared very irregularly.
The first four numbers only appeared in their due
time,—April, May, June and July, 1812. There were
two numbers issued in 1813 (October and December),
three in 1814, only one in 1815, one in 1816, another
in 1820, and the last in 1825, being a Letter to the
Marquis Wellesley,—in all, only sixteen. A perfect
copy, containing all the numbers issued, is very rare.
One day, last year, meeting my friend, Jasper Jolly,
LL.D., crossing the Court of Honour, of Leinster
House (for Leinster House is one described in France
as "Entre Cour et Jardin"), I mentioned to him that
I had often wished to see the Library he was arranging
and cataloguing as a gift,—a noble gift,—to add to the
National Library. "Come, then, with me (said he)
to the garrets of Leinster House, and there you shall
see me at my daily work."

We came up beautiful back staircases of stone,
admirably lighted, till we were in the covered garrets,
which were the ordinary (and only) sleeping rooms of
Leinster House.

They appeared low, from being so large. Many of
them must have been double and triple-bedded. There
were several filled with Jasper Joly's books. Coming
to a narrow passage, well lighted with shelves on each
side, "There (said Joly) is the gem ; the principal

treasure, as I deem it, of my Library. There is the Periodical Literature of Ireland." "Have you got (said I) ' The Milesian Magazine '?" His eye brightened with triumph as he led me to the shelves and took down a large brown paper parcel, and, untying the cords, he took number after number of the Magazine, throwing them down like a dealer of playing cards. " There's number one, number two," and so on until he had gone through the whole series. " All (said he) in their blue jackets, with the plates or etchings in their several states."

One reason assigned for the rarity of the complete work is, that no bookseller dared to sell so libellous a work. The two first numbers only have the names of the printers and publishers ; the others are without. I have heard that the Wrestling Doctor carried the numbers loose in the ample pockets of his great-coat, on sale—" To Friends, price 5s. To Enemies, 2s. 6d." There is no doubt, I believe, that he got a pension of £200 a-year by the Duke of Richmond's influence for his ridicule of the Catholic Committee in his " Barny, Barny, buck or doe." Shortly before his death he asked the Rev. Dr. Spratt, Provincial of the Car-melites, the great Apostle of Temperance, in succession to Father Mathew, to return him the copy of the entire work he had given him, as if he repented of his biting satire. Dr. Brenan dwelt in Great Britain Street, in French Street, and then in Great Britain Street again. He died, as I am informed by his grand-son (Henry James Loughnan), my friend and brother barrister, in 1830, who also gave me the date of his birth.

------

N

# INDEX.

## PERSONS AND PLACES.

THE END.

www.ingramcontent.com/pod-product-compliance
Lightning Source LLC
Chambersburg PA
CBHW030115030726
47498CB00007B/2393